Suspicion Stalks the Moor

Also by Josephine Pullein-Thompson

STAR-RIDERS OF THE MOOR
FEAR TREKS THE MOOR
RIDE TO THE RESCUE
GHOST HORSE ON THE MOOR
TREASURE ON THE MOOR
MYSTERY ON THE MOOR

(with Diana and Christine Pullein-Thompson)

BLACK BEAUTY'S CLAN
BLACK BEAUTY'S FAMILY

Josephine Pullein-Thompson

Suspicion
Stalks the Moor

Illustrated by Glenn Steward

HODDER AND STOUGHTON
LONDON SYDNEY AUCKLAND TORONTO

British Library Cataloguing in Publication Data

Pullein-Thompson, Josephine
    Suspicion stalks the moor.
    I. Title   II. Steward, Glenn
    823'.914[J]   PZ7

    ISBN 0-340-36677-X

Published by Hodder and Stoughton Children's Books,
a division of Hodder and Stoughton Ltd,
Mill Road, Dunton Green, Sevenoaks, Kent TN13 2YJ

Photoset by Rowland Phototypesetting Ltd,
Bury St Edmunds, Suffolk

Printed and Bound in Great Britain by
T.J. Press (Padstow) Ltd, Padstow, Cornwall

Contents

1

A horse on a boat?

It was the beginning of the summer holidays and, as we rode across the moor, we were all five cursing the rock-hard ground and the relentless sun which had blazed down from the cloudless sky, day after day, scorching the parched moor to ever deeper shades of brown.

Danny, a scowl on his tanned, gipsy face, was also cursing Jess King.

'Typical Jess, leaving her crash cap in the car,' he grumbled, 'and typical Mrs King, expecting us all to drop everything and search the whole moor for the trekkers.'

'Don't worry,' Huw, who was carrying the forgotten crash cap, told him soothingly, 'we'll probably see them on West Moor, but if we don't we'll go to the farm and ask Mrs Jackson which way they've gone.'

'Can't we gallop at all, Sukey? Not ever?' Angela Fletcher asked me, putting on her moaning voice. She was staying with us again and riding Bingo – a dark brown with a white face – who used to be mine until Dad took Snowman in exchange for an unpaid veterinary bill. I looked back at Angela, wearing jodhs and a dark green tee-shirt, she was as squarely built as ever and her straight, black hair was still cut in a fringe to frame her square face.

'You might as well gallop on the roads,' I told her.

'You can see for yourself how hard it is; think of the ponies' legs.'

'Actually there are still a few places where you can canter,' argued Chris, my younger brother, who believes in accuracy. 'Peaty places like the Chilmarth Woods.'

We crossed the road between Middle Moor and West Moor near St Dinas, a row of grim stone cottages with church, chapel and shop, which never manages to look like a proper village. Unsheltered by trees or hills, the winter winds lash it unrelentingly, but now the cottages with their watered gardens made a green oasis in the desert of scorched moor. Beyond the village, our view to the north was blocked by the cruel, craggy heights of Black Tor and to the south by the boulder-strewn slopes of Old Dog, but in between, looking straight ahead, we could see in the distance the ruined tower of Tolkenny Castle and the wooded slopes of St Crissy which marks the western end of the moor.

'There they are,' called Danny, pointing.

We all watched as the long, slow-moving string of ponies and riders gradually disappeared round the far side of Old Dog.

'I reckon they're doing the Pennecford trek today, then,' decided Danny.

'Why don't we go back to St Dinas? Then we'd have time to stop at the shop for ice-creams before riding down the road to meet them,' suggested Angela.

'I think we'd better cut across the corner, go round Old Dog the opposite way and meet them head on,' argued Huw.

'Yes, and we'd better trot or we'll miss them,' I said, falling in behind black Crackers, who was twirling and champing impatiently, despite the heat.

It grew hotter and hotter as we trotted single file along

the narrow, twisting path towards Old Dog. I patted Snowman's elegant white neck and apologised for making him rush about in the heat. He is a very polite and uncomplaining pony. When we first had him he was terribly thin and covered in warts but with endless feeds and the summer grass he'd fattened up a lot, and as he had settled down and become friends with Bingo and Joey the warts had miraculously disappeared. Bingo had been half-starved as a foal and he used to have a head that looked too large for his small, stunted body, but he now looks quite normal, though he'll never be a show pony.

All our animals are crocks or cast-offs; with two vets in the family you seem to collect them. Inky, our Scotty, has only one eye; Milly, our hairy monster of a dog, was found abandoned on a motorway by the police. But with Chris's Joey, a stout little dun with black points, it was the other way round; he was ill-treating his owners. Chris and I are very alike, people always guess that we're brother and sister. We both have small faces with small mouths and noses, brown eyes and straight fair hair. We used to look rather pale and feeble, but living on the moor has changed us; nowadays we're brown and wiry and look quite tough.

As the path led us under the towering heights of Old Dog, we suddenly heard shouting ahead. Danny immediately gave Crackers his head and whirled along the path and the rest of us followed. As we swept round the corner and joined the main track we came upon the trekking party, scattered all over the place and obviously in a state of disarray. One group was chasing a loose pony, another clustered round a rider sitting on the track, while several ponies had seized their opportunity to look for grazeable grass and were ambling over the heather, ignoring their riders' aids and cries of distress. Jess King, looking very tall on the Jacksons' Rufus, was shouting at two strangers, a boy and a girl, who held a white goat by the collar round her neck.

'No one but a complete idiot would tether a goat right across the track,' Jess was shouting aggressively. 'Didn't you realise the chain could trip a pony up? You must both be completely bonkers.'

'Oh lor', it's Mick who's come off,' said Danny in an anxious voice. 'He's hurt, and what are we going to do with this lot?'

I dismounted and joined the group of grown-up trekkers who were crowding round Mick. He was sitting up, but looked dazed.

'What happened, are you all right?' I asked.

'He hit his head, the crash cap came off,' explained a woman with long blonde hair, who was wearing a pink trouser suit.

'The goat took fright at the ponies and tried to bolt off, suddenly tightening the chain across the track,' added a grey-haired man dressed in jeans and a checked cowboy shirt.

'He didn't stand a chance, and the ground's like iron,' said a woman in jodhpurs.

'What do we do now?' asked a beefy young man with cropped hair. 'None of us know where we're supposed to be going, it's chaotic.'

'How are you feeling, Mick?' I asked, ignoring the rest of them. He gazed at me with dazed, unfocussed eyes.

'What's the time?' he asked. 'I must groom the ponies. We've got to tack up, the trekkers'll be here in a minute. What's the time?'

'He keeps on and on like that, I think we'd better send for an ambulance,' decided the woman in pink, looking round.

'Some hope; we're in the middle of nowhere,' observed the grey-haired man.

'It's all right, he's only concussed.' Huw spoke with authority. 'It happened to me once. You recover in a few hours, but they like to keep you in hospital overnight to make sure. They woke me up every hour all through the night, shining torches in my eyes.'

'We'd better round them all up and take them back to the farm,' I said.

'Oh no.' Jess stopped ranting at the goat's owners and came over. 'It's my only chance of a ride. We're only staying with Gran for a couple of days and all the ponies are booked for tomorrow.'

'What a shame, the kids have been looking forward to this for so long . . .'

'It's too bad. First there was that muddle over the caravan and now this . . .'

'There ought to be two instructors with a party of this size . . .' All the trekkers began to complain at once.

'There, you see, no one wants to go back. It's just not on,' Jess told us. 'Danny, you work for the Jacksons, you can take over. We're only going to Pennecford, having lunch at one of the pubs, and then going for a gallop on the headland where we found the birds at Easter.' Danny looked doubtful. 'I know the way,' he admitted. 'If I had a sensible pony I wouldn't mind, but Crackers is a bit of a nut. If they go racing past me he'll go raving mad.'

'Oh come on, he's not that bad. Look, I'll ride Crackers and you can have Rufus,' offered Jess.

'You know you can't,' Toby loaned him to me on condition that I was the only person to ride him,' Danny snapped at her impatiently. 'Could you come, Sukey? With two of us we could just about manage and we would be helping the Jacksons out; Mick wouldn't want to lose a day's trekking.'

'OK,' I agreed. I knew that the Jacksons, who are always short of money, might find it hard to refund the trekkers, who had probably paid for their five day's trekking in advance. 'Some of us take the trek on to Pennecford and some take Mick home.'

'Thanks,' Danny sounded relieved.

Angela and Huw were talking gently to Mick.

I began to round up the trekkers. I hate talking to strangers, but I put on the sort of voice the Jacksons use and said, 'Would you all mount, please,' to the near ones, and then I began to wave my arms and shout at the distant ones. Chris caught Arctic. Snowman and I picked our way across the heather to drag back one of the grazing ponies whose rider, a girl of about ten, was crying.

'He'll be OK once he's back on the track,' I told her. Danny was struggling to leg up a plump lady who was convinced she couldn't get into the saddle without a mounting-block; Chris was turning round one of the huge, wide, Highland ponies, pointing her in the right direction.

'I'll go last,' he called, 'and see we don't lose any of them.' Danny, assisted by an impatient and contemptuous Jess, had heaved the plump lady up. He mounted and led the way towards the Ruveland lane. I could hear Angela and Huw patiently telling Mick the time as they turned back and headed for Black Tor Farm.

'We won't be long,' Angela called over her shoulder. 'We'll catch you up.'

Ahead I could hear Danny explaining to the trekkers that Crackers was a bit of a nut and very hard to control so they *must* stay behind him. At the back of the ride I could hear Chris enquiring politely whether this was the plump lady's first visit to the moor. The tearful child, whose name was Emma, had cheered up a bit so I let go of Chester and told her to steer him herself. Then Jess, looking even longer and lankier than last holidays, rode alongside me. Her face, with its strong, arched eyebrows and jutting nose and chin, wore its usual dissatisfied look.

'Danny says we *have* to have lunch at some grotty pub called the Rose and Crown,' she complained. 'I don't see why we can't change to the Mariners' Arms; that's where *we're* staying. It's great, bang on the quay.'

'You're not staying with Mrs Hathaway this time?' I asked.

'No, my parents are here too, and four of us are a bit too many for poor old Great-gran. It would be OK if Danny and his mother weren't living in the upstairs flat.'

'What about Georgie? Isn't she riding these holidays?'

'No, poor old Georgie will never be any good, wrong shape. Look,' she went on, pointing down the lane, 'there are those silly twits with the goat again.'

They were grazing the white goat on the side of the track which leads to the disused tin-mine. The boy was tall and thin with an untidy mass of red curly hair, he wore jeans and a red tee-shirt. The girl was quite different, younger, smaller, with black, short, curly hair and a brown skin; she was dressed in shorts and a blue tee-shirt. I noticed that they both wore a mass of button badges; then they turned their backs and pretended not to see us. On the other side of the lane, opposite the tin-mine track, stands a pair of ruined, roofless cottages. They've been like that for years, but now I noticed a new gate and, looking over the stone wall, I saw that both gardens had been cleared of brambles, nettles and bracken. Some chickens scratched contentedly, and one patch had been fenced with wire-netting and planted as a vegetable garden. A tall, thin, shirtless man with a moustache was mixing concrete with a shovel.

'What an idyllic spot,' gushed the pink-suited trekker. 'Oh, how I'd love to escape here to all this peace and quiet. Bliss!'

'It's a bit rough in the winter,' I told her, 'snowdrifts and awful storms and even in the summer it's not exactly peaceful. I mean there's a drought and a water shortage and endless moor fires at the moment, and in the spring we had a rabies scare . . .' But pink-suit was gazing round with a rapt expression on her face and not listening.

'We're going on the road now,' Danny was shouting. 'Single file and keep in.'

'Keep in,' I repeated to all the trekkers near me. For a short way the road is tree-lined and was deliciously cool, but then, when we had passed Penhydroc where the Hamiltons live, we were back on the moor and it was

14

hotter than ever. We left the road and took the long straight track which leads down the side of the moor to Pennecford. It was very boring riding along the familiar track so slowly and the Jacksons' fly-spray seemed to have worn off, so as well as being scorched by the sun each pony had a huge cloud of flies buzzing round its head.

Jess, riding beside Danny, nagged him into trying a trot.

'We're going to trot. Are you all ready? Shorten your reins,' Danny roared at the trekkers in a sergeant-major's voice.

It was a very sedate trot but the results were nerve-wracking. Emma dropped her reins, clutched the pommel with both hands and burst into tears. The plump lady gave a small shriek and swayed alarmingly. Two people lost stirrups and hardly any of them seemed to know how to rise at the trot, but bumped about on their ponies' backs in a very perilous manner. I was leading Emma and giving rapid advice to all the trekkers near me. I could hear Danny telling the grey-haired man to keep his hands down and stop pulling himself up by the reins; Chris was saying 'Rise a bit faster Mrs Brown, you keep missing one.'

Then there were moans from people who had a stitch, and pink-suit said her stirrup leather was cutting into her leg. Danny slowed gently to a walk. The men all produced large handkerchiefs and mopped their faces, the stirrup loosers recounted their experiences, giggling nervously. I gave Emma back her reins and Mrs Brown told Chris that she was afraid she'd never get the hang of it.

I was pleased to see the end of the moor, and the gate and cattle grid which stop the cattle and ponies wandering down into the town. I was even more pleased to see the shady yard beside the Rose and Crown where the ponies were to be tied. Two metal baths full of water awaited the thirsty steeds and Danny knew where to find a sack of feed, a stack of plastic buckets and a collection of headcollar ropes.

'Mrs Jackson drops them in the day before,' he explained, as he began to ladle out feeds. 'Can you check that they've all loosened their girths,' he added, looking round at the trekkers.

The ponies had made a rush to the baths and were drinking deep, then they stood with dreamy eyes and dripping mouths before drinking again. I went round clipping headcollar ropes on to the headcollars that the Jackson ponies always wear under their nosebandless bridles. When all the ponies were tied to the rings in the walls and munching from their buckets and Danny had explained about Mick's fall to Mr Barret, the publican, who was serving drinks while his wife handed out Cornish pasties, sandwiches and packets of crisps to the queue of trekkers, there was a clatter of hoofs and Angela and Huw turned into the yard.

'How's Mick?' we asked.

'Still concussed,' answered Huw. 'Mrs Jackson made him lie down, but she didn't seem very worried.'

As soon as Bingo was watered and fed, Angela made a bee-line for the trekkers' queue. I joined the three boys in a shady corner of the pub lawn. All the tables and chairs were already occupied so we threw ourselves down on the grass and opened our lunch bags.

'Mr Jackson's furious with those Webbers,' observed Huw through a mouthful of chicken pie. 'Are they really squatters?'

'No, Mr Webber was made redundant and they've bought Tinners' Cottages with his redundancy money,'

Danny told us. 'They're living in tents while they're rebuilding. The boy's called Max and the girl Kelly.'

'What are they like?' I asked.

'I dunno, nutters by the look of them,' answered Danny, as Angela and Jess came over, munching enormous pasties and threw themselves down beside us.

'The trekkers were all asking about shopping. I said that I'd take them down to the quay in ten minutes and you'd look after the ponies,' Jess told Danny in a bossy voice, 'and that they all had to be back here by two.'

Danny scowled ferociously. 'You did, did you? Well you told them wrong then. When it's hot, Mick lets them shop till half-past two. Gives the ponies a rest in the heat of the day – and then there's the tide to consider.'

'Well I'll be a pony-minder,' offered Huw, 'I hate shops in hot weather.'

'So will I, because I'm broke as usual,' observed Chris.

Later, Danny instructed the trekkers that they were to be back at the Rose and Crown at two-thirty sharp and, led by Jess and Angela, they rushed out of the pub garden and took the narrow street which leads down to the waterfront and the shops.

'Peace at last. I don't know how Mick stands them,' said Danny as we settled down in the shade again.

At half-past two precisely, when we had collected the feed buckets and were bridling the last of the ponies, Jess marched the trekkers back into the yard.

'Everyone's here but Angela,' she reported. 'We arranged to meet outside the supermarket but she didn't turn up.' Jess looked round the yard. 'I thought she might have come back early.'

'Not Angela, I expect she's enjoying a *third* lunch somewhere,' replied Chris in his severe voice.

'She'll turn up,' Danny didn't sound bothered. He

addressed the plump lady in encouraging tones, 'Come on, Mrs Singer, there's an old mounting-block in the corner here and I'll hold Drummer while you climb up.'

We tightened girths, held ponies, and gave the less agile trekkers tactful shoves, until we had the whole ride back in the saddle. Then, as there was still no sign of Angela, I took Bingo's reins over his head and mounted Snowman.

'Do you think something's happened to her?' I asked Chris.

'No. After three lunches anyone would find that hill a bit steep. She's saving herself the climb,' he answered, as we jogged down the narrow street.

The ponies all seemed revived by their rest, but the trekkers were inclined to moan about being stiff or having sore legs, and then, as we came out on the quay where the fashionable Mariners' Arms looks across the cobblestones to the harbour, Angela came running up.

'Oh, you are an angel, Sukey,' she exclaimed, taking Bingo's reins. 'I meant to come up to the Rose and Crown, but then something *very* strange happened. I heard a neigh coming from that boat,' she pointed to a sturdy, black-hulled cargo boat moored beside the quay. 'Of course I went over to look, and when a man came on deck I asked him, very politely, what sort of horse he had on board. He was beastly; rude and really snappy, he said he hadn't one, that his boat wasn't built to carry horses. Then he told me to get lost. But I know I heard a neigh and I've been keeping watch.'

Danny and Jess had ridden on at the head of our cavalcade, but Huw and Chris had waited for Angela to mount. The four of us stared suspiciously at the boat. It was certainly large and solid enough to carry a horse in its hold, and not at all like the sailing-boats and the cruisers which usually fill the Pennecford harbour.

'I can't see why anyone should bring a horse here by sea, it's far easier by road,' objected Chris.

'And why should anyone deny having a horse on board?' asked Huw.

'Well he did, and I *know* I heard a neigh,' said Angela, settling herself in the saddle.

As we trotted briskly along the quay in pursuit of the trekkers the sound of our iron-shod hoofs striking the cobbles echoed round the harbour, and suddenly a neigh, a deep, powerful – though muffled – neigh, came from the bowels of the black – hulled boat.

We pulled up and looked back.

'You're right,' Chris told Angela. 'That's the only boat it could have come from.'

'But why on earth?' asked Huw. 'There's no tax on importing horses so smuggling them in is pointless.'

The trekking party had reached the ford and Danny was calling to us indignantly, 'Come *on*. I need some help; this lot are starting to chicken out. We need some experienced people in between them. Sukey, can you go last and make sure they all come over?' He turned back to the trekkers. 'Head for the white post on the far bank and leave the rest to the ponies. Come on, Mr Page, you follow me.' Danny and Crackers plunged into the water and began to splash their way across. Jess gave stout, dun Trudy a whack across her rump and she followed. The tide had turned and was going out quite fast, but, owing to the drought, there was much less water than usual coming down from the hills so the estuary looked tame and not at all the roaring torrent it can be in the winter and spring. Jess had persuaded most of the children on small ponies to follow Trudy and now the crop-headed young man and his girlfriend were following her. The

pink suit and Angela led another group over, but Mrs Brown and Mrs Singer were both dithering on the bank, saying that they didn't think they could manage it; behind them, Emma was in tears.

'Follow Chris,' I said in commanding tones to the trekkers and brandished my whip threateningly at the ponies, who, knowing exactly what they were supposed to be doing, ignored their riders' indecision and slithered down the bank into the water. I had just turned to grab Emma when there were shrieks from the ford.

'Look out, he's going to lie down,' Huw shot passed me and began to belabour Drummer, a sleepy piebald, who had decided to take a really cooling mid-river dip and was slowly folding his legs. As Huw drove Drummer on, I dragged Emma's reins away from her and, once he had his head, little Chester was only too willing to follow the other ponies over. He and Snowman trotted side by side, cooling us and themselves with the splash raised by their hoofs. The noise was tremendous, but not loud enough to drown Mrs Singer's shrieks of anguish or the laughter of the other trekkers watching from the far bank.

While Mrs Brown and Mr Page emptied Mrs Singer's water-logged shoes and tried to squeeze the worst of the water from the legs of her jodhs, Angela was telling Danny and Jess about the horse on the boat and the two neighs. Danny, made irritable by responsibility, was hardly listening. He swore at Crackers for twirling and then said, 'Probably an engine spluttering, or an echo from a pony neighing on this side of the estuary.' And then, looking round at the trekkers, 'Everyone ready? If we don't get on it'll be high tide and you'll find yourselves swimming on the way home.'

Mrs Singer began to shriek and Emma to sob at the

thought of swimming, but Angela and Huw calmed them with the information that the high tide was a good ten hours away and Danny was only teasing.

As we rode on towards the point, Jess, whose eyes had brightened at the prospect of a mystery, jogged up beside me on Russet.

'You heard the second neigh, Sukey, and *you* thought it came from the boat?' she asked.

'There wasn't anywhere else it could have come from,' I answered. 'It certainly wasn't an engine or an echo.'

'Then the horse *must* have been stolen,' Jess decided. 'A gang has nicked a famous showjumper and they're going to sell it abroad. It's obvious; the man wouldn't have denied having a horse on board unless it was stolen.'

'Hang on,' said Chris, who'd appeared on the other side of me, 'if they loaded the horse at high tide why haven't they put to sea? Surely no one would sit about all day in a harbour full of tourists with a stolen horse on board? It's asking for trouble.'

'They could be bringing a stolen horse *in*,' suggested Huw thoughtfully. 'I think that's more likely. Then either they just missed the high tide or the horse box was late, so now they've got to wait for the next high tide to bring him ashore.'

'You mean the poor horse has got to wait all day in that boiling hot hold?' asked Angela indignantly.

'Well, Pennecford isn't a proper dock with cranes for lifting horses in crates off ships,' Huw pointed out, 'so they must be going to walk him off and they can't do that except around high tide when the deck will be level with the quay.'

'Right, we keep watch tonight,' said Jess, 'from ten till about two.'

'I can't see Mum and Dad agreeing to that,' I objected.

'No, I don't think it would be very popular with my mother,' agreed Huw.

'Well I shall keep watch alone then,' gloated Jess, 'and if I'm in a good mood I may tell you what happened tomorrow. The room Georgie and I are sharing at the Mariners' Arms is rather a dreary little attic, but it looks out on the harbour. Danny,' she called. Kicking Russet into a canter she swept passed the trekkers, 'Danny, can we go back by the harbour? I want to identify Angela's suspicious boat.'

'No we can't,' Danny answered in blunt, uncompromising tones, 'Mick promised Mr and Mrs Page that they could see St Nechtan's, it's a rare Saxon church or something, and I'm not disappointing them.'

2

Getting even

When we delivered our weary, saddle-sore trekkers home that evening Mrs Jackson told us that Mick was asleep, but she seemed quite convinced that he would wake fully recovered and able to lead the trek next day.

As we watched Mr Jackson, Heather and Tracy help the trekkers unsaddle and turn out their ponies, Danny, less certain of Mick's recovery, decided that he would be at Black Tor Farm early next morning to see if help was needed and suggested that as Huw isn't allowed to ride on the moor alone, the rest of us should collect him from Penhydroc. Jess had begun her usual jeering. We've never been able to make her understand that the moor is a wild place and must be treated with respect; that if you walk or ride alone and have an accident the moor people have to make up search parties to look for you, so we ignored her taunts and arranged to meet at Penhydroc at nine-thirty.

It was another morning of dazzling sunshine and the promise of scorching heat as we jogged across the moor to collect Huw. He was waiting beside the sliprail which leads into the Penhydroc fields.

'Danny hasn't telephoned, he was going to if things got out of control at Black Tor,' Huw told us, 'but I think we'd better go there first, and make *sure* everything's all right.'

Angela began to moan about wanting to jump in the

24

Chilmarth woods, but Huw, who can be quite obstinate sometimes, said, 'We'll go there later,' and set off at a brisk trot towards the St Dinas road.

As we rode down the lane to the farm we could see a figure, which looked like Mr Jackson, cutting corn with a tractor and old-fashioned binder in a distant field, but the yard was empty of Jacksons and ponies. Several collies, too hot to bark, lay panting in the shade and a few energetic chickens were taking dust-baths. The back door stood open but no one answered my cries of 'Mrs Jackson.'

'Heather's down in the school taking a huge ride,' called Huw, 'shall we go and ask her?'

'Oh yes,' Angela agreed eagerly, 'we can jump the walls.'

'Only the low parts,' I told her, 'because of the ground.'

'You are a *spoilsport*, Sukey,' she shouted at me as we trotted down the first field and popped gently over the first wall.

'It's not Sukey, it's the ground,' Chris backed me up.

'And we wouldn't be jumping at all if Mr Jackson had proper gates and not ghastly barbed-wire contraptions that take half-an-hour to open and shut,' added Huw, leading for the lowest point of the wall between us and the moor.

Heather stood in the middle of the all-weather school and a collection of hot-looking children rode round, touching their toes.

'How's Mick?' I called to her.

'Great, quite recovered, though he can't remember the goat,' she answered, walking towards us. 'Dad's still furious.'

'Has Danny gone out with the trek?' asked Huw.

'Yes, one of the trekkers chickened out, too stiff and sore after yesterday. So we swopped the ponies round; Jess is riding Jupiter and Danny Russet. They're not far ahead of you, up the tor I think,' she added as she turned back to her ride and told them to prepare to trot.

'Jess *will* be pleased, she's been given a decent pony at last,' said Angela as we took the track which leads to St Crissy.

We rode slowly, looking up at the tor, our eyes searching the steep winding sheep paths and rocky heights for the trekkers.

'It seems dotty to take a collection of beginners up there,' observed Chris in his critical voice.

'Danny says Mick takes them up for the view and the thrill of the climb,' explained Huw. 'Apparently most people book for five days' trekking so they have to spin out the excitement.'

'There they are,' I called, pointing at the long file of ponies worming its way down a narrow, twisting path high above our heads.

We could hear Mick's voice shouting instructions; 'Lean forward, legs back; leave it to the ponies. Hands down, Mr Page; lean *forward*, Mrs Singer; you must give the ponies their heads.' He kept it up, looking back, calling over his shoulder, as he led the way down.

Jess saw us first. She said something to Mick, pushed past him on the narrow path, and cantered down the last stretch; she looked very at home on the chestnut Juniper.

'We've found some sick sheep up there,' she said, halting dramatically as she reached us. 'Well, actually two of them are dead. They're Jackson sheep, so you're to ride back and tell Mr Jackson at once.'

'Two dead. How many sick?' asked Chris.

'Oh I don't know, three or four; it doesn't matter.'

'Any idea what's wrong? Do we want a vet or just Mr Jackson?' I asked, stalling, because I didn't feel like taking orders from Jess.

Mick joined us at the foot of the tor, but he was intent on talking the trekkers down, so we waited in silence until the last one had reached the comparative safety of the moor, then he turned to me and said, 'I reckon the sheep up there have got hold of something poisonous; the ones that aren't dead are pretty sick. Could you tell our mum, Sukey? Ask her to phone your father *before* she tells Dad. Tell her that I say we'll lose the others if she doesn't get a vet up on Black Tor quick.'

'Right,' I said, turning Snowman. 'And it's a few sheep that want treating, not a whole flock?'

'Two dead and four sick to date,' answered Mick with a sigh. 'Let's hope it's not catching.'

'I'll come with you, Sukey,' Chris and Huw both spoke at once.

'You won't need me then,' decided Angela. 'I'll go on with Jess and Danny.'

Forgetting the hard ground, we raced back to the farm. Skirting Heather's school, jumping the walls, we whirled into the farmyard. The back door still stood open, the house was still deserted.

'Mrs Jackson,' I yelled at the top of my voice, but only the chickens cackled.

'Perhaps she's gone shopping,' suggested Chris.

'We could try the caravan site,' Huw called over his shoulder as he bustled Minstrel across the yard, towards the field where the caravans stood in a square, each on its bald concrete slab.

'Mrs Jackson,' I yelled, and from the far corner caravan came an answering shout. We cantered over, the caravanners all seemed to be out; at least there were no people or cars to be seen, only lines of washing and bulging black rubbish sacks testifying to their existence. Mrs Jackson, wearing a navy-blue nylon overall and a shower cap, appeared in the doorway.

'Mick's not been took bad again?' she asked.

'No, it's the sheep,' I explained. 'We didn't see them, but we met Mick and he said two were dead and four very sick. He told us to tell you and ask you to send for a vet quickly; he thinks they've eaten something poisonous.'

'Oh dear, if it's not one thing it's another,' lamented Mrs Jackson, standing, wet mop in hand. 'I suppose you didn't see my husband about as you came through?'

'No, and Mick told us especially that we were to find *you*,' explained Huw, who could see that Chris and I were embarrassed at having to emphasise the need for a vet.

'Such an expense, and if they're all going to die there's not much sense in throwing good money after bad,' dithered Mrs Jackson.

'Mick said if you could get the vet there quickly, he thought he could save the others.' Huw spoke in his quiet, persuasive voice.

'I don't know, I really don't; the animals are my husband's business . . .'

'Mum, if Mick said telephone for a vet we'd better do it.' Tracy Jackson's head, newly blonde and with the latest in Afro hairstyles, appeared round the doorway of the next caravan. 'I'll run up to the house, shall I?'

'I don't know what your father will say to all the expense,' wailed Mrs Jackson. And Tracy, who seemed to think this meant yes, jumped down the steps, pulled off her rubber gloves and, calling over her shoulder, 'One of you had better come and tell me what to say,' set off at a brisk run for the farmhouse. We followed and I shouted the surgery number at her as she disappeared inside.

'Isn't it amazing that the Jackson children are all so sensible when they have such dotty parents?' asked Chris. 'I mean Mick's only just left school but he's running a trekking centre, Danny says he does the bookings and the accounts and writes masses of letters.'

'My father says successful men have unsuccessful sons,' said Huw, his long face rueful. 'He looks at me and Felix very gloomily sometimes; he says we've no "push". I think he's more hopeful about Toby.'

'But your brother Felix is brilliant,' I began, and then Tracy called for instructions. 'Two dead, four very sick, probably poisoned,' I answered. 'All up on Black Tor. We'll go and find them and be there to act as guides. Tell Dad it's really urgent; Mick says so.'

'Your dad's tied up, miles the other side of Crookhampton, so your mum's coming instead,' Tracy came through to the back door. 'She's dropping everything and starting now.'

We said goodbye to Tracy and rode back to the tor, jumping the walls and stopping for a moment to tell Heather the bad news on the way. We took the path up Black Tor – there is only one suitable for a party of trekkers – and braced ourselves for a horrible sight as we climbed. We came upon the sheep suddenly, on one of the little plateaus, usually grassy but now bald and burnt brown. The two dead sheep looked very dead, they lay sprawled, their lifeless carcases already appropriated by two huge clouds of avid, buzzing flies.

'Ugh!' I turned to the four living sheep. They looked decidedly mouldy. They lay with glazed eyes, panting despite their shorn coats, and obviously feeling very ill.

'I hope Mum puts the skids on or this one will be dead too,' observed Chris.

Huw had dismounted and was brushing the flies from the face of another of the sheep. 'It's awful not being able to help.'

I looked back across the moor. A land-rover was bumping down the farm track, but it wasn't one of ours.

'Oh lord, Mr Jackson's on his way,' I announced. 'He's going to be even *less* pleased when he finds the hated vet is Mum. All the moor farmers are male chauvinist pigs, but he's one of the worst. I hope he leaves that Australian gate open for her. Good, he has,' I reported.

Mr Jackson had reached Black Tor, and vanished below the overhang, when I saw one of *our* land-rovers coming down the track from the farm.

'She's in sight,' I announced.

'And *he's* practically here, I can hear him puffing as he climbs,' Chris muttered at me gloomily.

Mr Jackson arrived too out of breath to speak. He took off his ancient hat and mopped his red and shining forehead as he looked down at his sheep.

'Poisoned,' he said with conviction, when he had inspected the dead and living in turn. 'Deliberately poisoned, that's what's done for them. *And* I know who it was.'

We looked at each other doubtfully. 'You mean someone gave them *poison* on purpose?' I asked disbelievingly.

'Arh, some'll do anything to get even.' He looked at the four panting ewes, 'Poor old things, they'll go the same way.'

'There's a vet coming,' I said nervously. 'Mick said we were to send for one.'

'She'll bring an antidote, I expect,' Huw was trying to sound confident.

'Vets, what do they know?' Mr Jackson's voice was full of contempt. 'All they learn at college is to talk big and hand out a lot of expensive drugs.'

Huw looked at us, wondering how we were going to react, but I wasn't going to show any sign of annoyance. Dad says it takes seven years to be accepted in real country places like the moor, and Mum says it'll be fifty years before the moor farmers realise that women vets are capable of treating large animals and not just budgies and poodles.

Chris, who *was* looking a bit annoyed, said, 'Why don't we ride down and meet Mum, Sukey? Then she could come up on Snowman and Joey could carry her bag.'

I was about to protest that this sounded a great plan for everyone but me, who would then have to walk up, but another look at the sheep stopped me. With their lives at stake my legs didn't really matter.

'OK,' I agreed as I mounted, and we set off down the rocky path as fast as we dared.

'Transport,' announced Chris when we came upon Mum, already puffing as she tackled the lower slopes.

'Mr Jackson thinks the ewes have been deliberately poisoned,' I told her as I lengthened Snowman's stirrups.

'Here, Sukey, you can have Joey and act as bag carrier,' Chris offered his reins.

'Are you sure?'

'Yes, I'll wait by the land-rover. I've had enough of looking at those poor sheep and of listening to Mr Jackson.'

When we reached the plateau, Huw, who is always polite, said 'Good morning, Mrs Ashworth,' and took Snowman. Mr Jackson only made a grunting noise. As Mum bent over the sheep, I dismounted and opened her bag in readiness. Mr Jackson followed her as she went from one sick ewe to another, examining their eyes and gums, observing their pulse rates and breathing.

'I don't need a lady vet to tell me my ewes have been poisoned,' he suddenly burst out in a very truculent voice. 'There's nothing you can do, better fetch your humane killer and put the poor old things out of their misery. I suppose they teach lady vets how to use them things.'

Mum straightened up and asked, 'What about the rest

of the flock; any problems? It could be sheep-dip, what do you use?'

'That's not sheep-dip, that's deliberate poisoning,' Mr Jackson answered contemptuously. 'I know who done it. That new chap at Tinners' Cottages. I went over and gave him a piece of my mind last night. Told him he had no business tethering goats all over the moor tracks. That we didn't want newcomers coming in interfering. But what he didn't like was when I told him that he didn't have no grazing rights on the moor. He tried to argue, but I told him that there had been no one living at Tinners' in the sixties when the new register was made. "Lapsed. Gone for good," I told him, "and there's nothing you can do." He didn't like that, so he got even with me, poisoning my ewes.'

'Malicious poisoning is a serious charge,' said Mum, looking in her bag. 'And what poison are you suggesting he used?'

'Rat poison, insecticides, weedkillers. They've come from London and could have brought all sorts with them. And animals will eat and drink anything when it's as dry as this.'

'Yes, you're right about the effect of the drought,' agreed Mum, arming herself with a disposable syringe and a phial, 'and if the new people are clearing out an overgrown garden, they *could* have dumped poisonous hedge clippings or weeds on the moor. But I can tell you that it's not rat-poison, nor yew, nor ragwort. As a matter of interest, when *were* they last dipped? Since shearing?'

'Of course they've been dipped since shearing, but I haven't been giving them sheep-dip to drink, have I?' demanded Mr Jackson.

'No, but if it was a very hot day and they weren't

33

watered just beforehand, half a dozen of the very thirsty ones *might* have been tempted to try a mouthful; it's happened before. Now, could you hold this one steady, Mr Jackson,' she went on. 'I want to give her a couple of shots that should help.'

'*Should* help. She'll be dead before night,' announced Mr Jackson gloomily, but he knelt down and steadied the ewes in turn as Mum injected them.

'Now, I'd like to take one of the bodies home at once, do a post-mortem right away and get the stomach contents and any affected organs to the analyst in Baybourne this afternoon. Then, if any of the rest of the flock develop symptoms, we'll know what we're treating,' said Mum in businesslike tones.

Mr Jackson carried one of the dead sheep down on his back and put it in our land-rover, then he said he was going to find his brother-in-law, Geoff, who would help him get the living sheep home to the farm. Mum told him that she'd be in touch as soon as she had any news.

'What do you think it is, and can you cure them?' Chris asked anxiously as soon as Mr Jackson had driven away.

'I think it's sheep-dip, but Mr Jackson's not going to accept that it was his own fault easily; he's looking for a scapegoat, trying to blame Mr Webber,' answered Mum.

'But you're not certain?' asked Chris.

'No, not until I hear what the analyst finds.'

'So they could still die?'

'Yes,' Mum didn't sound too depressed. 'You can't win them all. I've given what I hope is the antidote and shots of pain-killer; now we must wait and see. Let me know if you find any more in the same state,' she called as she turned the land-rover and drove away.

'Do you think Mr Jackson could be right about the

34

Webbers?' asked Chris as we rode on towards St Crissy and the castle.

'No, people who are fond of animals wouldn't dream of poisoning sheep on purpose,' Huw answered firmly, 'and they seemed very fond of their goat.'

'They could have thrown hedge trimmings out without realising they were poisonous,' I suggested.

'Mrs Merton at the shop told my mother a bit about them. Mr Webber was made redundant but the money he was given wasn't enough to buy a proper house so he decided to buy Tinners' and do them up himself, as he's unemployed,' Huw explained. 'I don't think a *really* horrible person would want to come and live on the moor.'

We caught up with Mick and his trekkers in St Crissy. They had had lunch at the Rising Sun, explored the castle ruins, and now the greediest of them were eating cream teas while the others bought postcards, piskie brooches, ships in bottles and pots of heather honey at the souvenir shop.

We told Mick, who was minding the ponies in the pub yard, what had happened about the sheep and how everything now depended on the result of the post-mortem. We didn't say much about Mr Jackson because Heather and Mick always seem a bit ashamed of their father. We'd run out of conversation when Jess came bounding down the road.

'Hi, you've arrived at *last*,' she said. 'I can't think why you took so long, all you had to do was get a vet. Anyway,' she went on, giving us no time to reply, 'I forgot to tell you about the horse this morning when we were all fussing over the sheep, but it *was* on that boat. It was nearly midnight when these two men appeared and went on board. Then three of them led the horse ashore

and one went back on the boat, while the original two
hurried him across the quay and out of sight.'

'What did the horse look like?' asked Chris.

'Terrific, he was obviously a racehorse or at least a
thoroughbred; you know, tall, fine head, spindly legs, no
hairy fetlocks, but a posh mane and tail. Very well-bred
looking. He pranced along with a tremendously arched
neck, I think he's a stallion, but I couldn't see well enough
to be certain.'

'What colour?' I asked.

'Dark brown or black, or very dark bay, that sort of
colour, but difficult to tell exactly in the light of the street
lamps. Definitely not grey or chestnut, or roan or any
fancy colour. He had white socks on three of his legs and
some sort of white marking on his face.'

'What were the men like?' asked Huw.

'Just ordinary. Well, one was very small,' Jess tried to remember, 'and he wore trousers and an anorak. The other one wore a tweedy jacket, I think. They looked like the normal people you see around here; not holiday-makers.'

'You didn't see a horse box?' asked Mick.

'No, I suppose it must have been waiting on the road.'

'It does sound as though they were smuggling the horse in,' said Huw thoughtfully.

'Unless the horse box was late and so they missed unloading him on the earlier high tide,' said Chris in his cynical voice.

'Oh, come on, of course they were smuggling him in. Why on earth would they chose a pathetic little port like Pennecford if they weren't smuggling?'

'But *why* smuggle a horse in?' asked Huw, his long face puzzled. 'They're not like dogs and cats, they don't have to spend six months in quarantine, do they?'

'No, I don't think so. Not from Ireland anyway,' I answered. 'Dad sometimes wishes that there was a short quarantine because the Irish horses quite often come over with strangles, which they have in a mild form, but they give it to the English horses, who all get it badly.'

'*Ireland*,' shrieked Jess. 'Of course, that's it. Don't you see? He's been kidnapped, they're always kidnapping horses over there; he's a valuable stallion and he's going to be hidden somewhere on the moor until the owners pay the ransom.'

'They're not *always* kidnapping horses,' objected Chris. 'I can only think of two; there was Shergar, but that was ages ago, and then there was a Derby winner quite recently.'

'Easter Chance,' said Mick, 'but the ransom wasn't paid and the papers seemed to think he's dead. Pity, he

37

was a good horse and should have bred some good foals, but it was only his first year at stud so there won't be many of them.'

'Easter Chance, that's it,' Jess's bony face was alight with excitement. 'We're going to find him, outwit the kidnappers and send him back to stud. The worst of it is that I'm being dragged back to London tonight, but at least I can go to the library and find a photograph of him. You lot have got the exciting part, you must search the moor night and day until he's discovered. And I'll nag my mother night and day until she lets me come back.'

3

We need evidence

Next morning, we'd agreed to meet again at the Penhydroc slip rails. Danny greeted us with a scowl on his gipsy face.

'Jess is coming back,' he said, 'she's got round her mother. They're letting her stay with Mrs Hathaway instead of going to France.'

I groaned. 'How long for?' I asked, dismal at the news.

'Two weeks.'

'Don't be beastly, Sukey,' Angela snapped, as I groaned again.

'What's she going to ride?' asked Chris.

'Well she had a go at bullying the Jacksons,' answered Danny, 'but Heather said there was no way they could help, so now Jess is planning to buy a pony of her own. She says the local paper's full of them and she'll find something.'

'Good old Jess. I wish I was brave enough to do things like that,' said Angela admiringly. 'Oh I do hope she gets one; it's such fun when we all ride together.'

'Has she the money to buy a pony?' asked Chris as we rode towards the Chilmarth woods.

'She says she's got enough in the Post Office for a *cheap* pony, and she doesn't mind what it's like,' Danny answered. 'I tried to talk some sense into her about winter keep and paying for shoes and tack, but she just said I was wet.'

'Cheer up, Sukey,' Huw gave me one of his rueful smiles. 'Perhaps she'll spend the next fortnight trying ponies and we'll be left in peace.'

'If only we could find the stallion today, without Jess,' said Chris.

'Sukey, you must tell Huw and Danny about last night,' Angela prompted me. 'You were the one who was awake when your parents came back.'

'Well there was an accident,' I explained. 'We were all in bed when the police called both our parents out. When they came back they said it was rather horrible. A car had gone into a herd of ponies halfway down the Crooked Billet lane. It was a car full of holiday people and the driver was either drunk or going far too fast. They had to put down three of the ponies.'

'And it's so sad, two of them had foals,' added Angela in her moaning voice.

'What happened to the foals?' asked Huw.

'Well the new man at Quarry Farm, he's called Spalding, took over the Kitsons' ponies with the farm, so the police rang him from the Crooked Billet and he took the foals home in the back of his land-rover,' I explained. 'Mum said they were about three months old, which means they've learned to eat, so though it's really too early to wean them, they'll survive.'

'Dad said Mr Spalding was an odd sort of bloke, not at all the usual moorland farmer,' Chris took up the story, 'and very cagey but he did mention that he'd retired from business and was going to run Quarry Farm as a *stud*.'

'What sort of stud?' asked Huw.

'Dad said he became vague when they tried to pump him, but that he did say the foals would make companions for the young stock he bought in the autumn.' I answered.

40

'Well, what are we waiting for, let's go and have a look,' said Danny briskly.

We rode through the Chilmarth woods, ice-cream cool after the baking moor, and then crossed the road, weaving our way through a queue of holiday traffic, and climbed the steep slope of Menacoell, which means Stone of the Eagle. However hot it is, there is always a breeze on Menacoell and you can see for miles, but it was a depressing view, a sea of scorched grass and parched brown heather; even the trees were beginning to turn golden and orange as though their leaves thought it was autumn.

Huw looked and sighed, 'I do wish it would rain.'

'Mr Jackson says it's getting really serious. There's no grass left so the farmers are having to feed hay, which means there'll be a shortage this winter and prices will rocket,' Danny told us gloomily.

'And then there are the fires,' said Chris. 'Look at that black area over by St Crissy; that must have been quite a big one.'

'There was a worse one last night, between Weavers and Baybourne, they had three fire-engines over there,' observed Danny.

'And then there's not being able to have baths; I *hate* showers,' Angela complained.

'And not being able to water the garden,' added Huw. 'My mother's recycling the washing-up water.'

We followed the path round the top of the old stone quarry and found ourselves looking the opposite way, out across North Moor. Being lower lying, it was a slightly less depressing sight than Middle Moor. Mason's Bog had kept its evil green, and around it the heather had found enough water to flower normally, making a purple circle in the waste of brown.

Quarry Farm, stone-built with wall-divided fields, blended grey with brown, except for the green-painted roof of a huge Dutch barn.

'The grass on Mason's Bog must be dreadfully tempting to the ponies this year,' said Angela, as we slid down the steep escarpment to the moor.

We rode along the twisting path at a gentle trot instead of our usual brisk canter, and when we joined the main track which runs from the farm to the Crooked Billet we walked, for it was even harder, the last of the grass worn away by wheels, and the ruts and potholes newly filled with shingle.

'They're turning it into a road,' complained Huw.

'Well in the Kitsons' time it was hardly used except by their land-rover,' Danny pointed out. 'They even took their churns to the Crooked Billet for the milk lorry.'

'If this Spalding is hiding a kidnapped stallion he isn't going to want too much traffic,' said Chris.

'It looks fairly busy there now,' I observed, standing in my stirrups for a better view. There's a land-rover, two lorries and a horse box parked in the yard.'

'A posh horse box,' added Chris as the track brought us up to the yard gate and, beside it, a small wicket gate into the farmhouse's tangled garden with its hollyhock-guarded wall. There was a sound of hammering coming from the Dutch barn and a concrete mixer churning away in a corner of the yard. Our ponies were sniffing the air in an interested manner when a thin, high-pitched whinny came from one of the farm buildings. Snowman answered.

'Sounds like the foals,' said Danny, as two desperate-sounding voices called in reply.

'Poor little things, they sound so sad,' moaned Angela as we stood in a row looking over the gate into the yard.

If there were loose boxes they were of the old-fashioned type, for no heads looked out over half-doors. Our ponies were still giving fatherly answers to the shrill cries for help when a much deeper voice, giving a powerful full-throated neigh, joined in. We looked at each other with rising excitement. 'That sounds like the stallion.'

'That *is* the stallion.'

'You can't be certain without seeing him.'

We were all standing in our stirrups trying to see where the neigh had come from, when a sarcastic voice asked, 'Can I help you?' We turned and saw that a man had come out of the farmhouse and stood at the hollyhock-framed gate, eyeing us suspiciously. He was tall, rather bald and wore dark-framed spectacles; he didn't look like a farmer.

Unable to think of a reply, I stared at him stupidly. The

others seemed surprised into silence too, then Angela stammered out, 'We were – er – trying to see your horses.'

'Well your presence is exciting them, upsetting them; can't you hear?' asked the man in a cold, unpleasant voice. 'I don't want them upset, nor do I want posters nailed to my barn door and half-baked leaflets, written by people who know damn all about farming, put through my letter-box, so perhaps you'd go away and *stay away*. All right?'

We gazed at him in open-mouthed surprise.

'Posters on barns and leaflets through letter-boxes?' queried Huw.

'Don't bother to deny it, just get lost,' said the man. And then, in a less controlled voice, he shouted, 'Go on, do I have to tell you more than once? Scram.'

'We'd better go,' Danny gave the twirling Crackers his head and breaking into a canter led the way back along the track. Our hoofs were rattling on the rock-hard ground and I soon began to shout suggestions about slowing down, but Danny kept going until he had passed the turn for Menacoell, then he pulled up and we all gathered round him, talking at once.

'What a beastly man; he obviously had something to hide.'

'We were quite dotty, why didn't we tell him that we'd come to ask after the orphaned foals?'

'He took us by surprise; all I could think about was the kidnapped stallion.'

'We looked guilty; but what on earth did he mean about the posters and leaflets?'

'It's those nutty Webbers again, I'll bet,' said Danny. 'They've been putting leaflets against factory farming through every letter box in the village.'

'But he's not factory farming,' protested Chris.

'Doesn't look like it,' agreed Danny, 'but those kids are too daft to know the difference.'

'Oh dear, I hope we're not going to be blamed by all the farmers,' moaned Angela. 'If he hadn't been angry he might have shown us the foals. I was longing to see them.'

'*I* was longing to see the stallion. That's what we came for,' Chris pointed out. 'But if you ask me the poster and leaflets were just an excuse to get rid of us.'

'And I'm all for protests against factory farming,' Huw spoke with conviction. 'It *is* horrible and it ought to be banned.'

'But it's no good a couple of town kids going round telling the farmers what to do, it just puts their backs up,' said Danny, riding on in the direction of the Crooked Billet.

'What are we going to do now?' I asked. 'We can't go back there. If only we'd got a *glimpse* of the stallion.'

'I don't think we've done *too* badly,' argued Angela. 'We've found the farm and we've met the kidnapper.'

'No we haven't, we're just guessing,' Chris told her severely. 'We need evidence.'

'If old Frosty's about I think we should stop and ask him,' said Danny, 'there's a chance he might know what's going on.'

Mr Frost is the landlord of the Crooked Billet and though he isn't really a local person – he's only lived on the moor for four or five years – he likes knowing all the gossip and news and his pub is very popular with the farmers, especially in the summer when they want to get away from the hordes of holidaymakers in Pennecford and Redbridge. As we came into the lane we saw him, bushy-bearded, dressed in a bright red shirt and blue jeans, busily wiping the tables which stood outside the tiny white-washed inn.

'You'd better ask, Sukey,' said Chris.

'Yes, go on, Sukey,' the others agreed, making way for me. We all called 'Good morning;' and then, as he turned to look at the ponies, I asked, 'We were wondering if you know anything about the new people at Quarry Farm?'

'I can't say I've seen much of Mr Spalding, he's a widower, I understand,' answered Mr Frost, gladly abandoning his table-wiping. 'In fact we hadn't exchanged a word until the accident last night. Very nasty it was too, even your parents said they were glad of a drink after we'd cleared up that mess. But one of the lads who works for him *is* a regular customer, ex racing stable, name of Lennie. Of course we're getting a deal more traffic past here, mares going to the stallion as well as the builders' lorries; I don't want too much, it would change the character of the place, but so far it's been good for trade.'

'Have they had the stallion there long?' asked Huw, trying to make his question sound innocent.

'Long? No. It can't be more than two weeks since Mr Spalding moved in, and, from what Lennie was saying in the bar, the stallion arrived before they were ready for him, but it seems he's highly thought of and the mares have been coming in a steady stream even though it's so late in the breeding season.'

'Do you know the name of the stallion?' asked Danny.

'Well he's known as Billy, but he does have an official name too; one of those daft racehorse names, impossible to remember.' Mr Frost thought hard, 'Something Omen. No, I've got it, it's even dafter, No Omen.'

46

We rode on down the long lane towards the Redbridge to Baybourne road, feeling quite pleased with ourselves. At least we had enough information to placate a scornful Jess. Our only problem seemed to be getting a look at the stallion. Angela had managed to persuade us all that we wanted ice-creams in St Dinas before going our separate ways, so we rode slowly down the lane listening to the subdued splash of the stream and the plaintive baas of the grass-searching sheep, and discussing ways of identifying the stallion now that we were forbidden to approach the farm. Huw and Chris favoured disguises. Angela proposed that we sent one of our parents to visit the orphaned foals. Danny wanted to creep into the stable at dead of night, I proposed that we made friends with the ex racing stable lad, Lennie.

By the time we reached the shop in St Dinas we were all dying for our long-awaited ice-creams. We had dismounted and were standing outside, counting our money and calculating which sort we could afford, when the Webbers came rushing out.

'Oh thank goodness you're here,' said Kelly in a flustered voice, 'it's nothing but disasters to-day. My mother and I came shopping and found Mrs Merton lying with a broken leg, well, Mum thought it was broken and the ambulance men agreed. She was lying there in the store-room behind the shop and no one had heard her calling for help.'

'Poor old Mrs Merton,' said Danny sympathetically. 'Her only son lives in Canada; what's she going to do about the shop?'

'My father's minding it at the moment,' explained Max. 'My mother went with Mrs Merton in the ambulance and Kelly fetched my father and I was coming over too when I saw these cows in the lane.'

'What about our ice-creams?' Angela wailed despairingly.

'I told you, my father's serving,' Max snapped at her. 'He's carrying on until we hear from Mrs Merton, she's hoping they'll let her out once her leg's in plaster. It's the cows I'm worrying about now. They're staggering around or sitting at the side of the lane in really weird attitudes, I'm sure cows don't usually behave like that.'

'Sounds odd,' I agreed as I watched Angela hand her reins to Chris and make a dash for the shop.

'There shouldn't be any cows on the moor, well not milking cows anyway,' observed Danny. 'Mr Gardiner's could have broken out I suppose; were they Friesians – black and white?'

'No, brown and white. I don't think they can see properly.' Max's pale face below his tangle of red hair was looking very worried. 'I tried to ask Mr Gardiner about them,' he went on, 'but he only yelled at me to clear off. Then I stopped two tourists but they only spoke German, and then a whole party of ramblers came by; they agreed the cows looked peculiar, but they said they came from Bexley and didn't know anything about cows and that I should telephone the police.'

'Did you?' asked Huw.

'No, what would the police know about cows? They'd just arrest me as a hoaxer.'

'Things are different in the country,' Huw told him. 'But it does sound as though some of us had better take a look.'

'Cut across to Old Dog,' said Danny as we mounted.

'I'll chase you, if Angela ever comes out of the shop,' shouted Chris.

'In the Ruveland lane, outside your house?' Huw checked with Max.

48

We trotted briskly across the moor and, as we skirted Old Dog with the mid-day sun scorching down on us, I bitterly regretted my unbought ice-lolly. But, as we entered the lane and came face to face with a large, hairy, brown and white bullock, staggering along with a dazed expression, I forgot all about being hot and thirsty.

'Cows!' said Danny contemptuously, as we edged our way past the bullock.

'He looks drunk to me, do you think there's some fermented grain lying around?'

'There's another bullock coming down from the tin-mine, he looks even more peculiar,' I observed.

'And there's one down there, sitting in the ditch,' Danny pointed.

We gathered round the one in the ditch. He was sitting on his haunches like a dog and there was a dazed look on his white hairy face. The ponies backed away from him suspiciously, snorting their disapproval of such outlandish behaviour. I dismounted and waved my hand in front of the bullock's eyes. He didn't seem to see it.

'A vet?' asked Huw.

'I dunno,' Danny sounded doubtful. 'They look a bit like Mr Jackson's bullocks; I know he's got some about this size running on the moor.'

'And if they are Mr Jackson's he's not going to be pleased at having a vet two days running,' I suggested.

'You're right, he'll go berserk,' said Danny. 'If we had halters we could try to lead them back to the farm,' he added, looking round vaguely.

'We'd better not touch them, suppose it's rabies again,' I argued, remembering the scare we had had at Easter.

'Yes, it's possible,' agreed Huw, looking worried. 'I remember your mother telling us that there was a depressed stage *before* the mad stage which everyone knows about. I think we should get a vet, Sukey.'

I looked at Danny, who stopped cursing the impatiently twirling Crackers and said, 'OK, if there's a chance it's
rabies we've got to do something quick.'

'I'll go down to the telephone box, the one on the
corner by the road,' I decided. 'Will you keep guard and
make sure no one touches them?'

'I'd better get over to Black Tor and tell the Jacksons
what's going on,' said Danny.

'I'll stay on guard then,' agreed Huw.

I was trotting down the lane preparing my account of
what was wrong with the bullocks (Dad always com-
plains that the clients don't *think* before they start their
explanations) when round the corner from the road came
a land-rover. I was pulling in to the side when I realised
that the figure at the wheel was Mum.

'How did you know we needed you?' I demanded as

she stopped, 'I was just going to telephone.'

'About the "mad cows"?' she asked.

'Bullocks,' I answered. 'Who told you?'

'Some hikers saw them and telephoned the police. The police were worried that we might have another rabies epidemic on our hands and sent for me. I hope you didn't touch them.'

'No, we thought of rabies too,' I said, riding beside the land-rover as she drove on. 'Huw's guarding them; Danny's gone to Black Tor, he thinks they're Jackson bullocks.'

Mum groaned and whizzed on up the lane. I jogged behind, glad that it wasn't us who'd sent for a vet.

When I reached them Mum and Huw were both looking at the bullock in the ditch with concerned expressions.

'I've noticed that they all seem very thirsty,' Huw was telling her, 'the other two keep blundering into the ditch and trying to drink, they can't seem to understand that it's dried up.'

'Well it's not rabies, I'm glad to say,' announced Mum. 'Please, Sukey, could you fetch me a halter from the land-rover.'

I gave Huw Snowman to hold and ran for the halter.

'What do you think it is then?' I asked.

'Give us a chance,' she answered as she slipped on the halter and then gave me the rope. She looked in the bullock's eye and then took his pulse with two fingers, watching the rise and fall of his flank at the same time to see how fast he was breathing.

'Let's look at that one next,' said Mum, taking the halter off the ditch bullock and advancing on the nearer of the staggering ones. We were examining the third bullock, and Mum was still answering my questions with non-committal noises, when a clatter of hoofs and a burst of chatter signalled the arrival of Chris and Angela. As they turned into the lane I saw that they were leading Bingo and Joey while the Webbers rode.

'Hullo, how are things going?' asked Angela in a cheery voice. 'We couldn't make Max and Kelly walk all the way here, so we've been taking it in turns to ride. They're awfully good, they can practically rise to the trot already.'

'Are these the mad cows?' Chris asked in the sort of hushed voice you use in church or hospital.

'No, they're sick bullocks,' I answered quietly, trying not to disturb Mum in the middle of her examination, 'but it's *not* rabies.' Then, as a land-rover came rattling up the lane, I added, 'Mum, Mr Jackson's arriving.'

He got out and stood looking sorrowfully at the bullock in the ditch. Then he took off his hat and mopped his forehead and, as he came over to us, the sorrowful look was replaced by one of red-faced anger.

'It's those Webbers again,' he told Mum. 'Same thing as the sheep, poisoned, that's what they are. I'm going to the police this time, I've had enough.'

I looked round nervously and was glad to see that Angela had taken her pupils farther down the lane. Mum was shaking her head.

'It's not the same poison,' she said. 'We've got staggering gait and impaired vision among the symptoms this time.' She looked at us, 'Have the Webbers started painting their cottage yet?'

'No, you can see, it's still a ruin,' I answered.

'They were painting the door of their goat stable yesterday,' said Chris. 'I know because Max is speckled with green paint and I asked him why.'

'Could you pop in and see if you can find any paint-pots lying around?' asked Mum. 'And if there are bring them here, I'd like a look.'

'You reckon that they've been chucking out their empty paint pots, do you then?' demanded Mr Jackson. 'Just what you'd expect from Londoners.'

'It's possible,' said Mum calmly. 'You know as well as I do, Mr Jackson, that bullocks will lick anything, especially in a very dry summer like this one, with the grass burnt to nothing. It could be a newly painted fence, or a broken-up car battery that someone's dumped, or even lead-rich ashes if anyone has been burning old doors with dozens of coats of lead paint on them.'

Chris, carrying half a pot of green paint, returned with Danny.

'This is all there is, no empties lying around,' he said, offering the can to Mum.

'No, well that's not to blame, it's lead-free,' observed Mum handing it back. What about primer?'

Chris shook his head and Danny said, 'Looks like an old shed, second-hand, it's been painted before.'

'See any old car batteries lying around?' asked Mr Jackson.

'No, they've got it all cleared up and very tidy,' answered Danny. 'Looks better than it has for years.'

'Have they had a bonfire then?'

'Yes, in one of the rooms of the ruin,' said Chris, 'I noticed because I thought it was rather a good idea when the moor's so dry and everyone's afraid of fire.'

'And is the garden wall bullock-proof?' asked Mum.

'Yes, they've built it up all round,' answered Chris.

'Well, I'd like to find the source, but I'm certain that it is lead poisoning,' said Mum briskly. 'Luckily there's a good and comparatively new treatment . . .' she broke off as a shout came from Huw, 'The gate into the mine is open and there's another sick bullock up in the yard.'

Mum dismissed the fourth bullock with a glance, even I could see that he was a carbon copy of the other two staggerers, and began prowling round the tin-mine yard.

'You can see why they came in here,' she said, pointing to the weeds and grass growing among the broken cobbles and cracked concrete.

We scattered among the long-abandoned outbuildings and rusty machinery. Some of the sheds had collapsed completely, some had holes in their roofs or were tileless, with rafters bare to the sky. Only the main building, used by a part-time boat repairer, was being preserved. We wandered round peering through doorways and into courtyards until Chris shouted that he thought he had found it.

'In there,' he said when the rest of us joined him. 'A great drum half-full of dried-up red paint. You can tell the bullocks have been in because of the cowpats.'

Mum and Mr Jackson, unimpeded by ponies, rushed to see.

'That's it,' Chris announced their verdict, 'mystery solved. Next mystery – what's happened to my pony?'

'When last seen he was being ridden by Max,' I said, 'and Angela was instructing.'

'They're not bad, those Webbers,' observed Chris, patting Snowman who was blowing gently in his hair. 'They've got some rather dotty ideas, but I quite like them.'

'Massive doses of sulphate of magnesium; that's Epsom salts,' Mum was telling Mr Jackson as they emerged. 'It acts like a charm if you start at once. As they're so thirsty they'll probably drink it in gruel or milk, but if not we'll drench them. Then I give them shots of a chelating agent, it converts the lead in the body into a harmless substance which can be excreted by the kidneys. We have to keep the treatment up for several days, but I'd expect them all to make complete recoveries.'

'Do you want any help getting them home?' I asked.

'No thanks, love. I'm just going to give Mr Jackson all the Epsom salts I have in the land-rover and then he's going home to fetch his cattle-truck and some strong men,' Mum gave me a wink. 'Then I'll go over to Black Tor this afternoon to give them their shots of calcium-EDTA.'

'Right, we're off then,' said Chris, 'I hope there's some food at home, I'm really famished.'

We found Angela in the lane holding both ponies, while the Webbers performed exercises – round-the-world and touching their toes – at her command, and all headed for home.

4

A pathetic bunch of fusspots

'The sheep are a whole lot better, and Jess *has* bought a pony,' Danny telephoned quite soon after we reached home; we'd put the ponies away in the cool dark of the stable and were reviving ourselves with iced drinks.

'What's it like?' I asked, when I had shouted the news to Angela and Chris.

'Flashy chestnut, four white socks. Bit herring-gutted, Arab-looking, too well-bred for the moor. Mare, barely thirteen-two. She's OK,' he admitted grudgingly. 'Nice temperament and Jess says she's fast for her size.'

'Oh great! Good old Jess,' Angela was jumping up and down with excitement. 'Oh, I'm longing to see her, do you think one of your parents would drive us over there this evening?'

'You're joking,' Chris said sarcastically.

'Nine-thirty here,' I said as I replaced the receiver. 'They want to ride on North Moor again, in the hope of seeing the stallion. Jess has got the photographs.'

'I know you don't like Jess, Sukey; and Danny simply loathes her, but you have to admit that she's a really enterprising person,' observed Angela in a voice full of admiration.

Next morning we were in the yard, saddled, bridled and mounted, at precisely half-past nine, but there was no sign of our fellow riders. We waited, looking at our watches impatiently, for ten minutes before we heard approaching hoofs, and the crash-capped heads of Huw and Danny came into view.

'Hullo, she's not here then?' asked Huw, pulling up at the gate.

'Jess? No, we thought she was coming with you.'

'So did we,' answered Danny in weary tones.

'What happened then?' I asked.

'She was grooming poor old Goldilocks when I left on my bike to collect Crackers,' Danny explained, 'and she agreed to meet us at the junction of the Chideock and Pennecford tracks. *We* got there on time, but there wasn't a sign of her. We waited ten minutes and then came on, thinking she must have gone ahead.'

'I hope she hasn't been bucked off,' said Angela.

'We'd have found her or seen the loose pony,' Huw pointed out.

'Do you want to telephone?' I asked Danny.

'I suppose so, but Mum's at work and I don't want to worry Mrs Hathaway,' he answered, reluctantly sliding off Crackers. 'Someone hold this maniac!'

'I've loaned Patchy to the Webbers for this morning,' Huw told us as we waited. 'It seemed potty that they should be longing to ride and he should be standing in a field feeling bored and neglected.'

'They'll love him, he's so sweet and just right for beginners,' observed Angela as Danny reappeared, scowling ferociously.

'She started out on the pony five minutes after I'd left on my bike,' he announced, taking Crackers from me. 'She must have decided to go for a ride on her own and she wasn't bothered about leaving us to wait. Come on, let's go,' he added as he swung into the saddle.

'Well it doesn't matter to us. If she wants to go off on

her own, let her,' said Huw in an unruffled voice.

'But I want to see the new pony,' moaned Angela.

'And it upsets Mrs Hathaway. She's lived on the moor for years and knows that it's dead stupid to go off on your own, especially on a new pony,' explained Danny.

'And Jess has the photographs,' I reminded them, 'so even if we see the stallion we can't identify him.'

'Have you seen them, Danny?' asked Chris.

'I had a quick look, but they're not coloured photos, so we still can't tell if the horses are bay, brown or black. They're only good for comparing the markings; the white socks and the blaze.'

'That Shergar business was years ago, it won't be him,' Chris said with certainty. 'What about a canter up Penkevil? It's downland turf so it oughtn't to be too hard.'

'Oh yes, do let's,'' shrieked Angela.

Though the sun was blazing down from another cloudless blue sky, the morning was still quite cool. We all looked up at the great hump of Penkevil – which means Hill of the Horse – and were tempted.

'We'll get a good view of Quarry Farm from the top,' said Huw. 'We might even see the stallion being exercised. Oh, why didn't I think of bringing my father's binoculars, I am dim.'

The ponies had realised our intention, they showed their approval by prancing around, tossing their manes and cannoning into each other as they tried to get good starts.

'OK, everyone ready?' asked Danny, leaning forward and letting Crackers go. We swept up the hill, standing in our stirrups and urging our ponies on. Sheep scattered with horrified baas, grazing ponies threw up their heads and watched.

Snowman's not particularly competitive so, when the

hill slowed Crackers down, we didn't try to pass, but galloped shoulder to shoulder with him and Minstrel.

We arrived at the top, patting our puffing ponies and feeling light-hearted. Angela and Chris weren't far behind.

'Do you see what I see?' asked Danny gloomily.

I looked round and gave a groan. Across the top of Penkevil a chestnut pony with white socks was galloping towards us, with Jess's long legs waving as she kicked for all she was worth.

'Oh hurrah, it's Jess and the new pony,' shrieked Angela, waving.

They came to a dramatic halt a few metres from us.

'Hi, what do you think of Goldie?' Jess asked. 'I got her for a song because I managed to convince the owners that I was a good home. I said I had a really nice cousin called Danny, who was going to look after her while I was away at school.'

We all looked at the lightly-built, chestnut pony in shocked silence. She stood with hanging head and heaving sides, her coat dark with sweat, which trickled down her legs and dripped on to the ground.

'You've practically ridden her to death already,' said Danny sharply.

'Oh, come on. She's a bit unfit, but I'll soon put that right. I've been jumping her in the Chilmarth woods and got her going really well. I've built a couple of bigger jumps, yours were pathetically low.'

'Did you forget you were supposed to be meeting us at the end of the Chideock track?' asked Huw.

'Oh, sorry. Last minute change of plan; I decided to go jumping instead. You didn't wait for me, did you?'

'We said we'd meet there, so of course we waited,' answered Huw.

'Do get off Goldie for a minute, Jess, she's still puffing like a bellows,' moaned Angela.

'Loosen her girth and turn her head to the wind,' advised Huw, 'that helps to revive them.'

'Oh, you are a pathetic bunch of fusspots,' complained Jess, dismounting reluctantly. 'I don't want the sort of pony that has to be kept in cotton wool. What's the point of having one if you can't gallop and jump as much as you like?'

None of us bothered to argue. We stood watching Goldie in disagreeable silence. Then Danny asked, 'Did you bring the photographs?'

'Yes,' Jess fished in her saddle-bag. 'Here you are, I found them in horsy year–books in the library and cut them out when no one was looking.'

'Jess! You are *awful*,' Angela giggled, but she sounded rather shocked.

'Well, at least I've done something. You're all so wet. We'd never get anywhere if it wasn't for me.'

'We have found a stallion at Quarry Farm,' Chris reminded her coldly as we passed the cuttings round.

Both horses had been photographed as Derby winners, as they were led in by proud owners. Easter Chance's owner was plump, he wore a morning suit, top-hat, and triumphant smile. I studied the horse carefully. He had that long, narrow white marking down his face which, for some strange reason, is called a 'race', and three small white socks. The off hind was the only leg without one.

'He's bright bay with black points,' Jess told us. 'I read that in the same book.'

'It's absolutely essential that we get a look at the Spalding stallion,' said Huw, handing a cutting back to Jess. 'Did Danny tell you he's supposed to be called No Omen?'

'Yes, Danny told me everything, including how you all trotted away obediently the moment the kidnapper told you to scram.' answered Jess in a contemptuous voice.

'You can't call him the kidnapper until we've proof that he's got the right stallion,' protested Chris.

'I can,' Jess was prepared to argue so I interrupted quickly.

'Look, we must make a plan. It's no use hanging round and hoping for a glimpse of the stallion because the Webbers have made it easy for Mr Spalding; he has a good reason for telling us to keep away and clear off, and he knows five of us by sight . . .'

'Disguises,' said Angela, 'we could dress up as gipsies.'

'He doesn't know Jess,' I went on, 'and my plan is that while the rest of us create a diversion round the front of the farm, she creeps in at the back and has a quick look round the stables.'

'Great idea,' Jess accepted the challenge without hesitation. 'Why don't I fall off? Then you could be chasing about trying to catch a riderless pony and, if I'm caught in

the farm, I'll say I'm looking for a telephone. I'll blub a
bit and say I've hurt my arm, my horrid pony's galloped
away and that I want Mummy to come and fetch me.'

'It's not a bad idea,' said Chris, frowning as he tried to
think of snags.

'It could be dangerous if these people *are* kidnappers,'
observed Huw.

'Terrific!' said Jess. 'Only if I'm kidnapped too you'd
better go straight to the police; I don't trust you lot to
rescue me. Think of the headlines: GIRL FOUND BOUND
AND GAGGED ON LONELY MOOR. And I'll be on the telly, of
course.'

'Do be sensible Jess,' pleaded Angela.

'I'm worried about Goldie. Supposing she doesn't go
in the right direction or she dodges us and sets off for her
old home?'

'She won't go back *there*. Don't worry, she'll follow
your ponies,' Jess answered confidently as we started
down Penkevil.

We parted at the foot of the hill. Jess had picked the
spot where she intended to fall off; it was close to the
boundary wall and at a point where only the width of one
field separated the moor from the farm buildings.

'I'll wake Goldie up, get her on her toes, so that she
really belts after you,' called Jess as we rode away, and
looking back I could see her holding the tired pony on a
tight rein and kicking with her heels until she produced
an irritable prance.

'Poor old Goldie, I'd hate to belong to Jess,' said Huw,
who was also looking back.

'Just at the moment I'd hate to *be* Jess,' observed
Angela with a shudder. 'I wouldn't go creeping into that
farmyard alone; you've got to admit she's brave.'

Danny had ignored the usual path from Penkevil

because it would lead us towards Masons' Bog and the moor's northern exit; he was following a winding little sheep path which ran close to the farm's boundary wall. We had a ride round three sides of the long field, which stuck out into the moor at a right-angle to the main square of farm land. Jess had only to climb the wall and cut across the field to the corner of the yard by the Dutch barn.

'Oh, she's done it; she's fallen off,' called Angela suddenly.

'I hope she's all right. It looked very realistic,' added Huw.

'Goldie's waiting for her,' said Chris. 'That's going to mess things up. She's waiting for Jess to get up and remount.'

'Probably glad of the rest,' observed Danny, without looking round.

'Don't shout so,' I told the others, 'Voices carry on the moor. I was looking across to the farm, watching for the moment when an enraged Mr Spalding would emerge.

'Jess has given her an almighty whack on the rump,' Chris reported in a lower voice. 'She's taken the hint, she's following us, but very slowly.'

As we came round the end of the long field and turned back towards the farm, we joined the main track which leads from Northcombe to the Crooked Billet, passing Masons' Bog and the Quarry Farm gate on the way.

'No land-rover, he must be out,' Danny sounded relieved.

'There's bound to be someone there,' I said, standing in my stirrups as I tried to get a good look at the yard.

'No one who knows us,' Danny insisted.

'I wouldn't be too sure. The ex racing stable lad may

have gone to fetch something in the land-rover,' argued Huw, looking round cautiously.

We had almost reached the house and the farm gate, when Goldie put on a spurt and came trotting after us.

'Loose pony,' we shouted at each other in unnecessarily loud voices, delighted that our feeble plan was actually beginning to work.

'Whoa, pony.'

'Where can the rider be?'

'I hope there hasn't been a serious accident.'

'Can you catch the pony? Head her off,' we called to

each other in theatrical tones. We milled round Goldie, colliding as we made wild grabs at her reins. We kept up the charade for as long as we could, but then Goldie refused to be chivvied round any longer, and stood with her head hanging and a dejected expression, longing to be caught.

Huw dismounted and tried to cheer her up with a handful of pony nuts and a sympathetic pat.

'Now we must look for the rider,' I announced loudly.

'Can't see a sign of one anywhere,' bawled Danny, standing in his stirrups and shading his eyes with one hand as he looked across the moor.

Angela tried to say something and then collapsed into a fit of giggles. I was wracking my brain for some way of prolonging the diversion. There was no sign of Jess, we mustn't leave too soon.

'I think we ought to divide into two parties and search in different directions,' suggested Chris.

'Perhaps some of us had better search and some wait here, in case the rider turns up,' suggested Huw.

'I wonder if the people at the farm know the pony? Perhaps she lives here and was coming home when we caught her,' said Angela, mastering her giggles.

'Brilliant idea,' Chris spoke softly, for our ears only.

'Quite true, that's probably the answer,' announced Huw loudly.

'Yes, I've never seen the pony about before, she must be new to the moor,' lied Danny.

I rode towards the yard gate, partly driven, I must admit, by a rather mean feeling that it would do Jess a lot of good if we got in first. The others followed me in apprehensive silence. But, as I opened the gate, I heard Jess's unmistakable voice, clear, confident and ringing, coming from the farm buildings.

'Yes, she tripped, put her foot in a rabbit-hole or something, and I went over her shoulder. I think I was a bit stunned, I didn't see which way she went and when I got up she'd vanished.'

The voice which answered was soft and Irish, we couldn't hear what it said. 'Yes, I expect she's gone home to Chideock,' Jess was agreeing. 'Well I can't walk all that way, especially with this leg, someone will have to . . .' At that moment Crackers twirled impatiently; the sound of his hoofs on the concrete yard gave us away and squeaky whinnies from the orphaned foals were followed by a deep neigh from the stallion. Our ponies answered and we looked at each other nervously.

'Better brazen it out,' said Huw. 'Anyone lost a chestnut pony?' he called. I was hoping that Jess had had time for a look at the stallion, I could imagine her fury if we had turned up too soon. But when she appeared from the farm buildings, limping badly, her face wore a triumphant expression.

'Oh, it's all right. Change of plan,' she called over her shoulder. 'Some people on ponies have caught her.'

'Hi, that's my pony,' she shouted at us.

'Are you OK? Did you fall off?' I asked, trying to sound like a stranger.

'Oh dear, you've hurt your leg. I hope it's not serious,' Angela sounded very concerned.

'It hurts, but it's not broken. I'll survive,' answered Jess briskly.

'Shall I give you a leg up?' offered Huw as he handed Goldie over.

'Thanks,' said Jess loudly. Then she mouthed at us almost silently, 'Let's get away quickly, before the boss comes back. I was right, it is them; I saw the stallion and it's him.'

66

I felt sick. Though we had been searching for the stallion I hadn't really expected to find him; it was as if some enjoyable but silly game of cops-and-robbers had suddenly become real. I waved the others out of the yard and shut the gate. Danny set off at a canter, leading us along the hard, main track, then swerving to the left and taking the path for Menacoell. He didn't stop until we reached the steep bank which leads up to the quarry. Then we all started asking questions at once.

'What happened?'

'Did you get a look at the stallion?'

'What did that Irish bloke say?'

'Did you get right into the stable, Jess?'

'Of course I did, that was the whole point. I told the bloke who was grooming the stallion that I'd fallen off and wanted to telephone my mother. He was quite friendly. He said that the boss was out, there was no-one in the house, but if I could hang on a minute until he'd finished doing the horse, he'd take me in to telephone. Suited me, being allowed to stand there checking up on the horse. He's bright bay with black points, three white socks and that narrow blaze thing down his face. He's exactly like the horse in the photograph. He's Easter Chance, there can't be any doubt about it. All the police in Ireland are looking for him, but he's here on the moor and *we've* found him.' She finished jubilantly.

The rest of us sat there with doubtful faces. Angela spoke first.

'What do we do now?' she asked. 'Tell the police?'

'Yes of course, and pretty swiftly. We're not going to let people who kidnap horses get away with it,' answered Jess. 'Which is the nearest police station?'

'Redbridge,' I answered, 'but I think that we ought to double-check that it's Easter Chance. I mean bay with

67

black points is a very common colour. We must be absolutely *certain*.'

'I am certain. I saw him, I tell you he's exactly like the horse in the photograph. What more do you want?' Jess demanded.

'OK, he looks like a horse in a rather blurred photograph, we could tell them that, but we can't burst in and tell them we've found Easter Chance.'

'Oh come on, it's not just the photograph. I watched him being unloaded from a boat at dead of night, remember?' protested Jess. 'Isn't that fishy enough for you?'

'I agree with Jess, but I would like to see the stallion for myself,' said Angela.

'Yes, we need a second witness.'

'Another identification,' Danny and Chris backed Angela up. The real point was that none of us trusted Jess, I thought. She was the sort of person who sees what she wants to see and she had decided that Mr Spalding was guilty.

'You've had days to identify him, you were just too cowardly,' sneered Jess.

'That's not true,' Chris rebutted the charge of cowardice indignantly.

'Could we talk it over with Mum or Dad?' I broke in. 'Vets know about thoroughbreds, where they are registered and that sort of thing. I know that they're not like ordinary horses, they're all listed in the Stud Book; you can check up on them.'

'And while we're checking up the kidnappers will escape, or someone else will realise what's going on and claim the reward,' objected Jess.

'Is there a reward?' asked Danny doubtingly.

'There's always a reward, the insurance company gives it,' Jess snapped impatiently.

'You see, mares are going to the stallion and he's standing under the name of No Omen, so No Omen must exist,' I pointed out.

'I don't see why, you can easily change a horse's name,' argued Jess.

'Not a thoroughbred's,' I stood my ground. 'They are registered as foals. And before the breeders send a mare to a stallion, they check up on all his relations. Some of the pedigrees go back for centuries, it's called studying bloodlines.' I knew I was explaining it badly and wished I had listened to Dad's lectures on racehorse breeding properly; he's always going on about the Darley Arabian and the Byerley Turk.

'And you mean all the foals from the mares who are going to him now will have to have No Omen registered as their sire?' said Huw thoughtfully. 'And, as no one's ever heard of him, they won't be anything like as valuable as if their sire was Easter Chance. I think we should consult someone before we go to the police. Will either of your parents be at home?'

'It'll be lunch-time by the time we get there,' I answered, 'with luck at least one of them should be.'

'It won't take long to consult,' said Huw, all of us looking at Jess.

'Oh all right. If you're all going to be so boring and difficult we'll call in at Marston on the way to Redbridge. But if your parents don't turn up, I'm going on to Redbridge police station on my own,' she said.

When we reached Church Farm my heart sank, for the yard was empty of land-rovers and Jess immediately began to nag.

'You said your parents would be home, what are we going to do now?'

'We can have lunch,' Angela told her cheerfully.

'I'll see if there's a note,' said Chris, dismounting and letting the dogs out of the office. 'No, nothing there,' he reported as Milly and Inky frisked round us, grinning through their beards.

We were all sitting under the apple tree in the front garden, eating and drinking in a reasonably contented manner, when with a couple of cheerful toots on the horn, Dad's land-rover came down the road. Chris got up and went to open the yard gate, and Jess, swallowing down a sandwich, ran after him.

'Mr Ashworth,' she began the moment he climbed out of the land-rover, 'we want to consult you. We've found the missing . . .'

'Can it wait five minutes?' asked Dad. 'I've had an exhausting morning and I'm covered in cow. I *must* have a shower.' He looked at me and Chris. 'Could you kids possibly make me some lunch? Cold meat, scrambled eggs, whatever there is.'

'But Mr Ashworth, this is urgent,' Jess pursued him into the house.

'Is anything going to die or burn down in the next five minutes?' asked Dad. 'If not it can wait.'

As I went in to collect Dad a lunch, Jess stormed out.

'Some people only think of themselves,' she complained angrily.

Chris giggled. 'I'll fetch Dad a cold beer, Sukey, that'll put him in a good mood,' he said, disappearing into the cellar.

'I love potato salad,' announced Angela, who'd followed me into the kitchen. 'Can't I have just one slice of ham, Sukey? There's masses there.'

When Dad reappeared with damp hair and wearing a clean shirt and jeans, we invited him into the garden and set a tray of food and drink before him.

'You are marvels,' he said grabbing the beer and taking a gulp. 'That's better, and I've drowned the smell of cow with some of Mum's carnation soap. Now, what's your problem?' He looked at Jess as he started on his ham.

'We've found Easter Chance, the Derby winner, who was kidnapped in Ireland,' Jess announced in a dramatic voice.

'We're not absolutely sure that we've found him,' I added hastily, in an attempt to tone down Jess's statement, 'but Mr Spalding's stallion at Quarry Farm looks very like a photograph of Easter Chance.'

'Jess is the only one who's seen him, the rest of us got chased off,' added Danny.

'We know he came to Pennecford by boat and was unloaded at midnight; that was what made us suspicious,' explained Angela.

'We thought you'd know about the Stud Book and how to check his description. Some of us feel we ought to have more proof before we go to the police; what do you think?' asked Huw.

'Here's the photograph.' Jess produced the cutting from her shirt pocket. 'The stallion at Quarry Farm is exactly like it in every detail. It *has* to be him. I think we should go straight to the police. And I'm prepared to go on my own,' she added, 'if the others are going to chicken out.'

'Isn't the Spalding stallion standing at stud?' asked Dad.

'Yes, and Mr Frost says that a lot of mares are being sent to him though it's so late in the year,' answered Chris.

'And what's he *supposed* to be called?'

'No Omen,' we all answered at once.

'Well then, for a start, let's get an official description of

No Omen,' suggested Dad. 'If he turns out to look nothing like the stallion who's standing in his name, you'll certainly have a case. I know criminal substitution of horses in races happens occasionally; you run a fast horse in the name of a slow one, which means far better odds from the bookmakers, back him heavily and win a fortune. But I can't see the point of substituting one stallion for another at stud.'

'Well, supposing he *is* Easter Chance,' said Huw. 'We know he was kidnapped, but the owners refused to pay the ransom, and the kidnappers are stuck with him. They could kill him, but it would be an awful waste, so they decide to send him to England, stable him in a fairly remote place and use him as a stallion under another name. Perhaps some people could be told about the kidnapping and would be prepared to pay high stud fees in the hope of breeding another Derby winner.'

'Not bad,' said Dad, chomping away at his salad. 'I think the best thing we can do is to telephone Weatherby's, they're responsible for the Stud Book and can give us detailed descriptions and, possibly, the blood groups of both horses.'

'Blood groups! That would be proof.' Chris sounded excited.

'Not necessarily; it's usually negative proof. You can say this foal *cannot* be the produce of that mare and stallion, or this foal *could be* theirs, but never this foal *is* theirs.'

'But if the two stallions had different blood groups, it would be easy,' observed Angela. 'That's great; I knew we needed an expert.'

'And how do we get hold of these Weatherby people?' asked Jess impatiently.

'They're based in Northamptonshire. If you can wait

until I've finished my lunch I'll phone them,' offered Dad. 'I think they might be prepared to give rather more information to a vet.'

'Ice-cream, Dad? Coffee?' I offered, hoping to hurry things up.

Dad telephoned from the office, and we all crowded into the doorway to listen.

'I'm Donald Ashworth, a veterinary surgeon, practising in the West Country,' he told whoever was at the other end of the line. 'I've had a query about the possible substitution of a thoroughbred stallion. Yes, well at the moment it's only local gossip and I thought a few facts from you might clear the whole matter up. Yes two descriptions. The missing Derby winner, Easter Chance, and a stallion called No Omen. And blood groups,

would you have a record of them too? Yes, I'll hold on.'
Dad looked at us. 'They're being very helpful,' he said.

We waited. I was beginning to feel sick again.

'Yes; ah, I see. Then we'll have to work from the descriptions,' Dad went on, while we waited impatient and baffled. 'Full brothers? Both out of Lucky Lil by Marsh King,' he was writing it down. 'Yes that does complicate things. Almost identical then, except for these ermine marks and they're on the near hind. Right. Yes I've got the ages, but as you say teeth are not entirely reliable. And you'll send me the photocopies right away? I'll give you my address.'

'They're full brothers,' we said, looking at each other.

'And almost identical. Then probably he is No Omen,' observed Angela in a disappointed voice.

'If he is, why bother with a boat?' demanded Jess. 'They've obviously swopped the brothers round, but it'll be that much harder to prove.'

Dad put down the receiver. 'How much of that did you get?' he asked.

'They're full brothers,' I answered. 'Same dam, same sire, and they look almost identical.'

'What about the blood groups?' asked Chris.

'They don't have complete records yet, there aren't enough laboratories to cope and there isn't one in Ireland where both these horses were foaled. There is a slight variation in the shape of their white markings and Weatherby's are going to send me photocopies of the drawings made by the breeder when the foals were registered. But the most spottable difference is the ermine marks on the near hind white pastern: Easter Chance has them, No Omen doesn't.'

'And what on earth are ermine marks?' demanded Jess in an irritable voice.

'Black spots on a white marking,' explained Dad, 'and their exact position will be shown on the photocopy. They've promised to send them first class post this afternoon.'

'Thanks, Dad,' said Chris.

'Yes thank you very much, Mr Ashworth. I'm not sure where it all leaves us, back to Quarry Farm with our magnifying glasses, I suppose,' said Huw.

'Oh, all that proving every detail is a dead waste of time,' argued Jess. 'All we've got to do is tell the police. Then, if we do turn out to be wrong, which you've got to admit is jolly unlikely, they can do the apologising.'

'Here, *we* have to go on living on the moor,' Dad protested. 'I don't think one ought to make accusations against neighbours unless one is absolutely certain of one's ground. I'd wait till you have the photocopies, then you'll be in a position to make an *informed* judgement.'

We could all see that Jess was too obstinate to be swayed by Dad's advice; she was convinced that she knew better. I decided to end the discussion.

'Any idea where Mum is?' I asked Dad, as I piled the dirty glasses on his tray.

'Yes, there's been a serious fire on the other side of Redbridge. A farmer was burning stubble and the whole thing got out of control. Crossed the road and swept through his neighbour's pig unit. Nasty. Mum was called to sort out the survivors.'

'Ugh, poor Mum, poor pigs,' I said, picking up the tray.

'I hope you're all being really careful about not starting fires. The whole of the moor is tinder dry and ripe for a colossal disaster.'

'Really Dad, we don't smoke, we don't burn stubble, we're not camping and we never throw broken glass around. How do you think *we're* going to start a fire?' I heard an indignant Chris demand as I went into the house.

I bundled everything into the dish-washer and then ran out to the yard, where I found the others gathered round Jess and arguing fiercely.

'It's boiling hot and the ponies need a rest. Bingo's exhausted,' said Angela.

'And it would be potty to turn up at the farm again so soon; it would be bound to make them suspicious,' Chris pointed out.

'Well if you're all so yellow, I'll go on my own,' threatened Jess. 'I'm not going to give them a chance to get away.'

'Don't be daft, they've got lots of mares booked, they're coining money; they won't go unless you stir things up,' Danny told her.

'And I've *got* to go home. I told the Webbers to bring Patchy back at three and if I'm not there they won't know where to put him,' explained Huw. 'Do be sensible, Jess. We'll all go over tomorrow or the next day.'

5

Too late! They've got away

As Jess refused to wait for the photocopies of the markings to arrive, we decided on a compromise, and swallowing her endless insults that we were wet and spineless, we all agreed to meet on top of Penkevil next morning, armed with new and brilliant plans for getting into Quarry Farm and identifying ermine marks.

However, when Chris and Angela and I reached the top of the great down on our puffing ponies, there were only two riders waiting. Huw was surveying the moor through a huge pair of binoculars, Danny came riding to meet us.

'No Jess?' Angela looked disappointed. Danny shook his head. 'Haven't seen her this morning, she must have started really early. Now she knows her way round the moor I don't think she wants to ride with us any more.'

Chris and I looked at each other and I could see that he was relieved to be Jess-less too.

'But she *agreed* to meet us here,' moaned Angela.

'That doesn't count for much with Jess,' said Danny as Huw handed him the binoculars.

'Take a look. It's all very busy down there. The concrete mixer's hard at work and they seem to be building something. The land-rover's in the yard, the horse box is missing and there's no sign of the stallion, but I did get a glimpse of Patchy.'

'Patchy? What's he doing on North Moor?' I asked.

'I've loaned him to the Webbers again, they said they had a great day with him yesterday. They seem to go miles, but very slowly, as they take it in turns to walk and ride. Their parents have told them to lay off the chicken farmers, so they're rescuing hedgehogs from cattle grids instead.'

'Rescuing hedgehogs?' Danny gave a contemptuous snort and handed the binoculars to Angela. 'They must be cracked.'

'No, I don't think so,' answered Huw mildly. 'It seems that hedgehogs fall through the gaps between the metal bars of the grids and as those holes underneath usually have straight brick sides, the poor old hedgehogs can't climb out and starve to death. All that needs to be done is to put a slanting board in the deep ones, so that the hedgehogs *can* climb out. Obvious really.'

'Did they think of it?' asked Angela admiringly.

'No, they got the idea from some wildlife society,' answered Huw, 'and they're going round the moor with the boards.'

It seemed hotter than ever, the air was heavy as though there was thunder about. I felt lazy, more like swimming than riding, and a half-headache thumped behind my eyes. Only the thought of Jess's constant taunts made me ride over North Moor yet again.

'We can circle the farm and then if we don't see any horse activity we'll make for Chilmarth,' said Huw as we rode down Penkevil.

'Calling in at the shop on the way, to ask after Mrs Merton,' added Angela.

We had reached the main track and were about to turn towards the Quarry Farm gate, when Angela asked, 'Is that Patchy over there by the bog, or is it a brown and white cow?'

We all looked. 'A skewbald pony,' decided Chris, 'And I think the rider's waving.'

Huw unzipped the binoculars' case.

'Yes, it *is* Patchy, Max is riding him, but I can't see Kelly,' he told us. Then his voice changed. 'I think something's happened, he's waving and shouting.'

'Wind's from the south,' observed Danny, 'dead loss trying to shout against that.'

'You look,' Huw passed him the binoculars, 'I think something must be wrong.'

'Yeh, he looks really worried. I think we'd better get over there fast,' agreed Danny.

We set off at a brisk canter. When we came to the low-lying area near the bog, the softer ground turned the rattle of our hoofs to a thud. We could see Max plainly, he had stopped waving and was riding to meet us. He shouted again, but the words didn't reach us; then we were near enough and heard him say, 'Can you come, there's been an accident.' We rode on faster and then engulfed Patchy in our cavalry charge as we pulled up.

'What's happened? Is someone in the bog?' we asked, looking round for disaster.

'No,' Max shook his head. He was scarlet in the face and shaking. 'It's that tall girl, we found her lying by the cattle grid. She's hurt, she can't get up and the pony's badly hurt too; it's bleeding. Kelly stayed with them.'

'Jess?' we asked.

'I forgot to ask her name, but she rides with the Jacksons. She told me to get an ambulance and a vet, but I couldn't find a house or a telephone *anywhere*.'

'A chestnut pony with white legs?' asked Angela. Max nodded.

'If *Jess* can't get up then she is hurt,' I said. 'The nearest telephone's at Quarry Farm.'

79

'I'll go back,' said Danny quickly.

'So will I,' offered Angela. They were both shying away from the gory scene which awaited us, I thought. I didn't like the idea of it much myself, but I knew that Chris and I were more experienced.

'Ambulance and vet, then,' said Huw, 'and they call it the Northcombe exit.'

'OK, and I know the Ashworth number.' Angela turned Bingo and tore after Crackers.

'Will you be all right if we canter?' Huw asked Max, as the rest of us rode on.

'Yes, I'll hang on to the mane,' Max answered.

The northern end of the moor has no pretty villages or ancient ruins and no tors to climb, so there's nothing to tempt tourists; nothing but cattle, ponies, and curlews crying mournfully as they wheel high overhead.

We passed the bog, green-rushed and smelling disgusting, and kept going at a steady canter until Huw shouted, 'Slow up, I think Max is getting tired.' I looked back, Max was standing in his stirrups and swaying dangerously. I slowed to a gentle trot and then a walk.

'Two of us had better go on ahead and one follow slowly with Max,' I called.

'I'll go on,' Chris answered. 'You stay, Huw, or Patchy may try to follow Minstrel.'

The track had become dusty, leading through a flat stretch of grass eaten absolutely bare by the hungry animals. Then we could see the gate and the cattle grid, Goldie's hindquarters, and Kelly waving as she ran to meet us.

'Did Max find you? Has he sent for an ambulance? Jess keeps asking. Oh, I'm so glad you've come.'

'Everything's under control,' I said, dismounting and leading Snowman through the hunting gate beside the grid. Chris took both ponies' reins and began to tell Kelly what we'd organised. I went to inspect Jess. She lay flat on her back in the middle of the lane. 'Hullo,' I said bending over her.

'Hullo,' she opened her eyes. 'Oh, it's only you. I hoped it was an ambulance or a doctor.'

'The ambulance is on its way,' I said, 'where are you hurt?'

'It's my shoulder and chest. It's bearable lying down, just throbs, but it hurts like hell if I try to sit up.'

'Stay where you are then,' I told her, wishing I had an anorak to roll into a pillow, but we were only wearing tee-shirts. Chris had left Kelly holding our ponies and was looking at Goldie's forelegs. He made a face as I joined him.

'Look at those knees. And she's scraped a lot of skin off her side. Both knees had round bloody holes. The bleeding had stopped, and there were rivulets of dried blood down the front of the cannon bones and more blood on the road.

'They're deep,' I said, waving the flies away and crouching to look closer. 'There'll be awful scars.'

'They're full of grit. I wish we had something to bathe them with,' Chris looked round helplessly.

'And some fly-spray,' I added. My handkerchief looked reasonably clean so I folded it into a triangle and knotted it loosely round Goldie's leg above the worst knee, hoping that by covering the wound I'd keep the flies away. Then I unsaddled her while she stood utterly dejected, eyes half-closed, head hanging, paying no attention to what was going on around her.

'Our first aid seems rather pathetic,' observed Chris in his critical voice, as he unbuckled her drop nose-band.

'Well, they don't need the kiss of life. As Dad says

"Most of first aid is keeping calm and being supportive until the experts take over."'

I went back to Jess.

'Can you remember what happened?' I asked.

'Yes of course, I'm not dotty. I landed on my shoulder, not my head,' she retorted irritably. 'It's all your fault, I knew we ought to have gone to the police yesterday, then none of this would have happened. Now it's too late; I'm smashed up and they've got away.'

'What happened then?' I asked again.

'Oh, what does it matter *now*,' said Jess closing her eyes. But then she began to talk. 'When I arrived at the farm they were loading the stallion into the horse box. His legs were bandaged for the journey, so I couldn't see the ermine marks, but it was him all right. I thought the box would make for the Crooked Billet lane, so I set off in that direction, planning to hold it up where the lane begins; it's narrow there and out of sight of the farm. I was going to make the driver show me the ermine marks and then ring the police from the pub. But it all went wrong.' She stirred restlessly and winced. 'I wish that ambulance would get a move on, the ground's getting harder and harder.'

'What went wrong?' I asked.

'I got a bad start. The box turned this way. I chased it and I was gaining, but I didn't know there was a way out here and I didn't see the beastly grid. That idiot Goldie should have jumped it, but she just slipped and slithered the whole way over and then fell flat. I hadn't a hope,' she added closing her eyes.

Max and Huw arrived. Kelly was looking after Snowman, so I met them and told them the latest news. Huw dismounted and went to inspect the casualties.

'The stallion doesn't seem very important now,' he

said when he came back and took Minstrel from me.

Then Danny and Angela thundered up dramatically.

'We got the ambulance OK, but both your parents were out. I left a message on the answerphone *and* I told the nurse,' announced Danny. 'I told them to go to the trekking centre, becaue Mr Jackson was at the farm and he said he would come right-away and collect Goldie.'

'He was delivering a caravan which he's sold to Mr Spalding,' Angela explained, 'and as his land-rover's broken down he was towing it with his cattle-truck. How's Jess?' she asked, looking apprehensively at the still figure.

'She's hurt her shoulder and she's suffering from shock,' I said, 'I think she might have broken something. Goldie's knees are pretty horrible, I think she'll be badly scarred.'

'Yes, broken knees never really recover,' agreed Huw gloomily.

Chris began to tell Danny how Jess had seen the stallion being driven away in the horse box, and chased it.

'That's strange, we were certain we heard the stallion neighing, weren't we, Angela?'

'Yes, but there could be two stallions, they could have both brothers there,' suggested Angela.

Mr Jackson arrived before the ambulance. We watched his old cattle-truck bumping across the moor and we greeted it as shipwrecked sailors greet a lifeboat. He couldn't drive across the grid, for Jess lay in the way, so he left the truck on the moor side and walked through. He looked at Jess first.

'Where does it hurt, love?' he asked.

'My shoulder, there,' Jess pointed to the front of her shoulder, 'I can't sit up.'

'What about the other arm, how's that?'

'OK.'

'And your legs?'

'OK.' Jess wriggled them to prove it.

'Doesn't look too bad then. Most likely you've broken your collar-bone,' said Mr Jackson. 'I broke mine twice, once in a point-to-point and once schooling a green 'orse over fences. You'll soon be about again.' He went on to look at Goldie.

We began to feel less gloomy.

'Perhaps I shouldn't have bothered Mrs Hathaway so soon,' worried Danny. 'I thought I ought to tell her, and she said she'd phone Mrs King in France right away.'

'Oh you stupid little clot,' Jess opened her eyes. 'Now you have done it. I haven't even broken it to them that I've *bought* Goldie yet. My father will go raving mad.'

Mr Jackson was still shaking his head and pursing his lips over Goldie's knees when the ambulance came slowly down the lane. The two uniformed men inspected Jess, who had suddenly become silent. I explained about her shoulder or collar-bone and that it hurt her to sit up, but that her legs and other arm were OK. Mr Jackson told them how he'd broken his collar-bone, twice, following them as they fetched a stretcher and laid it beside Jess. They told him to take Jess's legs and while one of them took her head and shoulders, the other whisked the stretcher underneath her body so quickly she hardly had time to wince. They slid the stretcher into the ambulance and then, as Jess didn't seem disposed to talk, I told one of the men her name and address and age, and he relayed them to the hospital on the radio. Chris remembered to ask to which hospital they were taking her, it was Redbridge, and Angela climbed into the ambulance to say goodbye and wish her luck.

As Jess was driven away we turned to Goldie. Mr Jackson brought the cattle-truck over the grid and parked it in front of her, with just enough room to let down the ramp. Then we had to persuade her to walk up; painful step by painful step.

'You better travel with her, Sukey,' Mr Jackson told me as he and Danny prepared to lift the ramp. 'Don't want to shake her up, so I'll go round by the road. One of you boys can lead the grey home.'

'Kelly can ride Snowman if she likes,' I called through the closing gap of the ramp, 'if Huw doesn't mind leading her.'

'Oh, I'd love to, thank you *very* much,' answered Kelly in a pleased voice.

'Couldn't I ride Snowman?' moaned Angela. 'Then Max could have Bingo, Kelly Patchy and no one would have to be led.'

'No,' I said firmly for I suspected Angela of trying to take over Snowman as she took over Bingo last holidays.

'Here, Kelly had better have my crash cap.'

'Don't worry,' called Huw as Mr Jackson edged the old truck forward slowly and smoothly, 'I'll look after Snowman.'

Poor Goldie was no trouble. She drooped, looking utterly miserable and never moved a hoof or twitched an ear the whole way. At first I tried to comfort her with gentle stroking, but then I decided she really wanted to be left to suffer in peace, so I looked out through the open ventilation slats and tried to work out where we were.

When we arrived at Black Tor Farm a distraught Mrs Jackson appeared. As Mr Jackson climbed down from the cab and hurried to lower the ramp, I could hear her telling him that the man from the Ministry had kept his appointment at eleven, waited twenty minutes, then left, *very* put out. And that Geoff was trying to cope with the Thirty Acre on his own.

'You said you'd only be half-an-hour, Tom,' was Mrs Jackson's final reproach, 'and it's gone half-past twelve.'

Mr Jackson only mumbled in answer and I felt guilty that helping us had got him in this mess. But the sight of Goldie's knees, and a rather louder mumble that we had to get the young girl off to hospital, did seem to calm Mrs Jackson down.

'Take your pick of the boxes, and when you see Heather tell her we're taking the little mare at livery,' he told me and then hurried across the yard in the direction of the Thirty Acre.

Mrs Jackson had scuttled back into the house. The yard was full of small ponies, they were tied up in the pigsties, in the barn and to posts along the walls, but there was no sign of any humans. I looked in the new loose-boxes, two had small ponies tied up in them, several ponies to a box, two were empty. I picked the cleanest one and, fetching a broom, began to sweep it out. I was bedding it down in clean straw when Heather appeared, leading a young pony on a lunge rein. I hastily explained what I was doing and gave her Mr Jackson's message, but she wasn't really listening to me, she was looking with shocked horror at Goldie's knees.

'They're full of dirt and grit, better get the hose on them,' she said. 'You stand her on the concrete and as soon as I've put Monty away, I'll connect it up for you.'

Heather provided me with a very gentle trickle of water and told me to start at the hoof and work up the leg. Goldie winced and tried to retreat at first, but then she seemed to decide that I was doing her good. I was at work on the second knee when a land-rover swept into the yard with Dad at the wheel.

'Oh dear, you have made a mess of yourself,' he told Goldie, as he bent to inspect her knees. 'Do you know how it happened?' he asked me. I explained about the cattle grid and how Jess hadn't realised it was there.

'Poor old lady,' he addressed Goldie again, 'you are feeling sorry for yourself. We'll give you a pain-killer before we go any further. You're doing a great job, Sukey, keep it up,' he added.

Goldie was past caring and stood motionless when he plunged the needle into her neck.

'I don't like the look of this one,' said Dad, crouching for a closer look. 'We could have an open joint here. You say she belongs to Jess King?'

'Yes, but Jess is on her way to Redbridge Hospital, Mr Jackson thinks she's broken her collar-bone; Mrs Hathaway's trying to get hold of her parents, but they're in France.'

Dad gave a gusty sigh. 'Well I'll give her a massive shot of antibiotic, but I'm not making any promises. If we get an infection in that joint she's had it.'

Goldie had had her second injection, and Dad was bandaging a sterile dressing over the worse knee, when the riding party appeared, followed by Heather.

'Thank you so much, Sukey, I had a lovely ride,' said Kelly, putting my crash cap on my head.

'How is she?' asked Angela.

'Not too good,' said Dad straightening up. 'Well, I've done my best; now who's looking after her?'

'Mr Jackson said that you'd take her at livery,' I said looking at Heather.

'He didn't! He knows that Mick and I are run off our feet. The treks are fully booked for the next three weeks and I've all these kids from the caravans wanting to ride, as well as my local lot,' objected Heather indignantly.

'We really haven't time to nurse a sick pony. He's out of his mind.'

'The knees can be left as they are for a day or two,' said Dad, 'but she must be stabled, so someone's got to muck her out and make her bran mashes.'

I was about to say that I didn't see how we could get across the moor early enough in the mornings, when Kelly spoke up.

'We could do it,' she offered, 'Max and I could look after her. If Mr Jackson doesn't mind us coming round,' she added in a less confident voice.

Heather looked at Max, who was obviously older and stronger.

'Yes, we can look after her,' he agreed, 'If someone will tell us what to do. We know quite a lot about goats, but not much about looking after ponies.'

'I'll give you the first lesson on how to make a bran

mash now, in the kitchen, while I'm eating my dinner,' said Heather in a relieved voice. 'Danny, can you teach them how to muck out?'

'Yeh, I'll come round tomorrow morning,' agreed Danny.

I led the still drooping Goldie into her stable and fetched her a bucket of water; she took a couple of half-hearted sips when I held it up to her. Danny filled a small hay net.

'Well we'll leave it like that then,' said Dad. 'She can have bran mashes, hay and cut grass, no pony nuts or oats. One of us will pop in and see her tomorrow and no doubt the Kings will be in touch with me when they hear what's happened.'

6

Touch and go

After the accident, and Jess's insistence that we were too late and that the stallion had been taken to a new hiding place, it had seemed pointless to make any more plans to watch Quarry Farm. We agreed to meet at the Jacksons next morning, to exchange news and see if help with Goldie's nursing was needed.

The photocopies of the markings of the two stallions arrived in the post, but we didn't bother to take them with us, their appearance only made us feel more downcast, underlining the knowledge that Jess had been proved right and that we ought to have acted sooner.

The yard at Black Tor Farm was empty of Jackson ponies. We could see Crackers, Minstrel and Patchy tied up in the long, open shed, while Danny, Huw and the Webbers were gathered round the door of Goldie's loosebox.

'How is she?' I asked as we joined them.

'Feeling a bit better,' answered Danny. 'She's eaten half her bran mash and picked at a bit of grass.'

'Oh, they have swollen up,' said Angela, as we stood in the doorway staring gloomily at the two shapeless legs and distorted knees.

'They're boiling hot,' Kelly sounded worried.

'Mum's coming over to see her, and the bullocks, directly after surgery,' said Chris, trying to cheer them up.

'Danny, have you heard any proper news of Jess?' asked Angela. 'Sukey's rung the hospital twice but they only said she was "comfortable".'

'Yeh, Mrs Hathaway hired a car and went over to see her last night. She *has* broken her collar-bone, but she did something else as well, displaced it or something. That's why they kept her in overnight,' Danny answered. 'She's got to be X-rayed again and then, if it's OK, she'll be allowed out. The big trouble is Mr King,' Danny went on, 'He was in a real temper last night, blamed Mrs Hathaway for everything. I hope he's cooled down when he gets here this morning.'

'Poor old Jess, bad enough to have a broken collar-bone, without a cross father.' sympathised Angela.

'*She* asked for it, it's Goldie and Mrs Hathaway I'm sorry for,' snapped Danny as an elderly-looking blue van bounced over the lane's potholes and into the yard. A tall thin man with a drooping moustache, wearing jeans and a tee-shirt, got out.

'Can you tell me where the caravan site is?'he called.

'Dad, what are you doing driving that van?' The Webbers rushed at him excitedly.

'It belongs to the shop, but no one's driven it for years, not since Mr Merton died,' he explained. 'It seemed a good idea to get it back on the road. One of the caravanners has put in a gigantic order – enough groceries to feed six starving kids for a month – and I'm trying to deliver.'

'I'll show you,' Kelly ran to open the gate and then climbed into the passenger seat.

'Our cottage is never going to be ready for the winter,' announced Max glumly. 'Hardly any work's being done on it now Mum and Dad are both so involved with the shop.'

'But what will you do?' Angela sounded anxious. 'You

can't live in those tiny tents in the winter.'

Max shrugged his shoulders. 'We aimed to have the ground floor finished and put on a temporary roof. Then build the upstairs next summer; but nothing's going according to plan.'

The groceries delivered, Kelly brought Mr Webber over to visit Goldie. He made a face when he saw her forelegs.

'It's obscene; to have done that to a beautiful pony. Stupid girl should never be allowed to ride again,' he said vehemently.

'Poor Jess didn't know the cattle grid was there,' Angela protested, but Mr Webber was pointing across the yard to the far field, 'Who's that cutting corn with the incredible old binder?' he asked.

'Mr Jackson, of course,' answered Danny.

'He's always years behind the times,' added Chris.

'The trouble is that he hasn't the capital to buy his own combine harvester and he's always in too much of a muddle to book the contractor who goes round the other small farms,' explained Huw.

'Pity,' said Mr Webber, 'I could have done with some of his straw. Oh well, I'd better get going.'

'What does he want straw for?' asked Danny as the van bounced away down the lane.

'He said that the old-fashioned machines cut the straw very long and don't squash it into bales, so you can use it for thatching roofs instead of burning it,' answered Kelly. 'I think he was planning to help the farmer with the harvest in exchange for the straw to thatch our cottage; but it's no use if it's Mr Jackson.'

'Pity,' agreed Max, 'it would have been great if we could have bartered our labour for the straw. It's much more sensible to barter things than to bother with money, you don't have to pay VAT or income tax.'

'But if *no-one* paid VAT or income tax the state would have no money for unemployment pay or the National Health Service,' objected Huw.

'Oh, don't start a long boring argument, *please*,' wailed Angela. 'Can't we decide where we're going to ride; the whole morning's passing and we haven't done a thing.'

'Perhaps we ought to ride over to Quarry Farm once more,' suggested Chris. 'It's just possible that the stallion was being taken somewhere for the day and came back in the evening.'

'And Danny and I did hear that neigh, so there could have been two stallions there,' Angela agreed.

Kelly looked at Huw. 'If you're really lending us Patchy again we want to go over to the Northcombe cattle grid,' she said. 'In all the worry of finding Jess and Goldie we forgot about our hedgehog board, we left it lying around somewhere.'

'One of you could come with us on Patchy, but it means leaving the other one behind,' said Huw. 'We go too fast for walkers.'

'We need to take three more boards over, the grid's one of the deep ones,' explained Max. 'There are brick walls dividing it into four compartments, so you need four boards. The grids on the main roads are different, they're quite shallow and the hedgehogs can get out, but at St Crissy and Pennecford and Northcombe they're real traps.'

'We can carry boards,' Huw told him. 'Danny's the only one with a pony which needs two hands. It's up to you.'

The Webbers were still discussing which of them should come with us when Mum bumped into the yard. She jumped out of the land-rover and came bustling over, bag in hand, in a very businesslike manner. She was wearing green trousers and a green checked shirt.

'Bad news, I'm afraid,' she said, before she had even looked at Goldie, 'Mr King is in an absolute fury. Did *you* know that Jess had bought the pony without telling her parents?'

'Not at the time,' answered Chris, 'but she told us yesterday, after the accident; she said her father would go berserk.'

'Well she's right, he has,' said Mum. 'He told me that the pony was to be put down at once, that he won't be responsible for veterinary fees or livery stable charges after twelve noon today.'

We looked at each other aghast. 'You *can't* put her down, Mum.'

'Oh, poor Jess.'

'Poor *Goldie*. It'd be a crime, putting down a nice pony like that.'

'You don't mean she's going to be killed?'

'But why, Mrs Ashworth? Surely it would be more sensible to get her well and then sell her?'

We were all talking at once, but it was Huw that Mum answered. 'It's not as easy as that. From what Don tells me one knee joint is open, so we can't promise a complete recovery; then there is a chance of septicaemia, which could be fatal. Even a complete recovery is going to leave her with obvious scarring, which will reduce her value as a riding pony. From an economic viewpoint he has quite a lot of sense on his side, but I'm afraid he's really doing it to teach Jess a lesson.'

'He sounds a really horrible man.'

'No wonder Jess is like she is.'

'He *can't* have Goldie killed.'

'What are you going to do, Mum?' I asked.

'Give him a few hours to cool off, I suppose,' she answered, 'He might possibly change his mind when he's seen Jess. Have we a headcollar, could someone hold Goldie while I take a look at those knees?'

The Webbers were acting as nurses so we let them hold the unprotesting Goldie, while Mum inspected the knees and the rest of us discussed what could be done.

"I'll have her," suggested Angela rather uncertainly. "I don't mind ugly knees. I could look after her for the rest of the holidays and then she could live with your ponies in the term, Sukey.'

'What about paying for shoes and winter keep?' I asked, 'I thought you'd gone into all that with your parents and they had said no.'

Angela made her moaning noise, 'It's not fair. They spend masses of money on Sea Spray and Ian and Rob have both been bought windsurfers, but I'm not allowed a pony. But I could ring them tonight and try again,' she added optimistically.

'Mr Jackson would take her on and use her as a brood mare if she was a moorland pony,' said Danny. 'Trouble is that she's too well-bred to be left out on the moor all winter.'

'She's such a sweet pony, there must be some way out,' I was thinking hard, but my mind seemed hopelessly blank.

'Well, it's touch and go,' said Mum, straightening up. She stood back and looked at Goldie. 'It's a terrible pity, because I can see she's the sort of pony who'd give a child years of happiness, but, economics being what they are . . .'

'She was sold extra cheap because Jess was supposed to be giving her a good home,' Huw reminded us. 'Would that make a difference?'

'Yes, you may have something there. That may give me quite a useful lever,' said Mum thoughtfully. 'Well, another shot of antibiotic, and I'll do what I can for the knees. You keep up the good work with bran mashes and cut grass,' she told the Webbers, 'and we'll hope for the best.'

'Our turns are in a muddle,' said Max when the injection had been given, 'but Kelly really wants to stay with Goldie so I'm coming with you.'

We set off, Huw, Chris and I carrying the hedgehog boards. Angela said she was looking after Max and needed a free hand to grab Patchy's rein in emergencies.

As we rode we discussed Mr King and what we could do about Goldie if he *didn't* change his mind. We all became very depressed for no one could think of a solution. Then, half-way up the Crooked Billet lane we realised that we were weak with hunger, and stopped to eat our lunches. As we ate, we planned our next move. Unless Mr Spalding appeared, we were going to ride straight past Quarry Farm and on to the cattle grid. But if he was standing by the farm gate, then, as Huw said, it would be only polite to stop and thank him for letting us telephone for the ambulance and also to give him the latest news of pony and rider. If he wasn't visible on the outward journey we would call on him on the way back, which might give us an excuse to enter the yard and search among the buildings.

The hedgehog boards, the intense heat and the iron-like ground all combined to make most of us glad to ride sedately. Only Angela and Max seemed to have any energy left; they were schooling wherever the moor was flattish and fairly stone-free, with Max turning, circling and halting at Angela's command, and then trotting to catch up with the rest of us.

Quarry Farm seemed dormant and deserted. The horse box and the land-rover were both absent and there was no sign of life from the house or the caravan, and no neighs came from the farm buildings.

'Looks as though Jess could have been right. They heard we were on to them and scarpered,' Danny admitted reluctantly. 'Even the building blokes have gone.'

'Well, it *is* Saturday,' Huw reminded him.

'And the first day of the Redbridge Revels,' I added, 'But are they the sort of people who'd watch pagan rituals and hobby-horse dancing?'

Danny made a contemptuous noise, 'No, it's dead boring, always the same. Not that they'd know that.'

'The new girl groom might go,' suggested Angela. 'Mr Jackson said she was arriving yesterday, that's why he had to bring the caravan over in such a rush.'

'I like the fair, but we can never go on many things, it's too expensive,' I complained.

'Fire,' called Chris pointing away to our left, where, on the open moor north of Knapp Tor, a column of grey smoke spiralled into the dark blue sky.

'There always seems to be a fire somewhere at the moment,' observed Huw.

'Yeh, another three yesterday,' agreed Danny, 'but they were all on the moor and didn't do any damage, not like the one at the pig farm, that was really nasty.'

'What about the little animals; the mice and voles and things which live in the heather?' demanded Max in a truculent voice.

'Yes, it's horrible, frogs and toads and fledgling birds are all burned to death too,' agreed Huw.

'Luckily they're all the sort of animals who breed again quickly,' said Danny. 'They're like grass and heather which grow again in no time – gorse takes a bit longer.'

'That's not much comfort to them when they're going through a terrifying moment and dying,' Huw pointed out.

'But they've all got to die in the end,' argued Chris, 'I don't suppose it's much better if a fox kills you or if an owl swoops down and carries you off in its claws and then eats you for its supper.'

'Oh shut up, I like owls and now you're putting me off them,' protested Angela. 'Why does nature have to be so beastly?'

'I only like vegetarian animals,' said Max, 'but I expect if there was more space and lots of fruit and grass they might give up eating each other.'

'Doubt it, look how birds go on. Blackbirds pull worms out of the ground and eat them, thrushes crack snails' shells and eat them and swallows eat flies and insects as they fly around – and then cats eat the birds. It's just natural,' observed Danny.

We spent some time fixing up the hedgehog boards to Max's satisfaction, and it wasn't until we were mounting for the homeward journey that we noticed the change in the weather.

'The wind seems to have got up,' said Huw.

'And look at that huge cloud over St Crissy.' I pointed at the sinister purple blackness which had suddenly enveloped the western end of the moor.

'Looks as though we're in for a storm; it's coming this way,' observed Danny.

'Oh hurrah, I hope it simply pours,' shrieked Angela cheerfully. 'I don't mind how wet I get as long as the drought ends. Come on rain; perhaps we'll be able to gallop and jump tomorrow.'

'I *hope* the rain comes in time to put out that fire,' said Chris in a subdued voice. 'It's moving much faster now that the wind's behind it. Surely someone must have seen it and telephoned the fire-brigade?'

We forgot the storm cloud as we stared anxiously at the grey wall of smoke advancing across North Moor and, below the smoke, the curling tongues of orange flames, suddenly flaring up as they moved forward in greedy darts to new patches of heather.

'Yes, it's really got going,' agreed Huw, 'and it's making straight for Quarry Farm. I think we'd better get back there and see if they need help.'

'It's the only telephone, but supposing there's no one there?' I asked.

'Break in,' suggested Danny.

'But if there's no one there and the fire-brigade doesn't come the orphaned foals will be burned to death,' moaned Angela. 'Come on, quickly.'

We set off at a canter with Danny and Angela sharing the lead, but then there was a shout from behind. I looked back, Max was clinging perilously round Patchy's neck.

'Slow down,' I shouted, 'Max is about to fall off,' and I pulled up, silently cursing the fact that we had landed ourselves with a beginner just when we needed to ride fast.

Chris, who was next to Max, had gone to his aid and was shoving him back into the saddle.

'OK to go on?' called Danny impatiently.

'Yes, I wasn't ready last time, but I'm all set now,' Max answered.

We set off again, behind I could hear Chris giving Max advice, ahead I watched the advance of the fire with apprehension. The stretch of moor between it and the farm was growing smaller by the second. We reached the northern end of the fire; now we were downwind of it, the smell of the smoke was strong in our nostrils and the westward sky was veiled grey with it.

'Surely *someone* must have seen all this smoke,' Chris shouted to me, 'they can't *all* be at the revels.'

'I suppose Menacoell and Knapp Tor hide it from the road,' I shouted back in a cheerful voice, trying to hide the fact that I was beginning to feel afraid. When we had ridden past the farm earlier the fire had seemed a couple of miles away, now there was only about one hundred metres between it and the farmhouse and it was gaining speed all the time. The flames were low and creeping on the bare, cropped moor, but when they found fuel in a patch of heather or clump of gorse they exploded into a raging blaze. I wondered what would happen when they reached the house; the garden was full of sun-dried plants, rows of bean-poles and pea-sticks. The Kitsons' old rabbit and ferret hutches would fuel the flames until they were powerful enough to devour the house. The yard was full of timber, the barns full of hay and straw. We *had* to get the animals away before the whole place went up. But how? I began to visualise the boundary wall. When Jess had done her falling off act she had had to climb over it, there had been no gates, no broken-down gaps, just a long high wall enclosing the whole farm. Snowman, Minstrel and Crackers could jump it, but not the smaller ponies, not the foals.

We reached the farmhouse; Danny had flung himself off, chucked his reins at Angela, burst through the wicket gate and was thundering on the door knocker, before the rest of us had pulled up.

'There *can't* be anyone there,' Huw told him after a few moments of banging.

'I'll try the back,' Danny vanished round the side of the house, then reappeared, 'It's locked too. We'll have to break in. Telephone's in the hall.'

'We'll check up on the animals,' I called as Huw went to help Danny. I opened the yard gate. Angela and Huw had hitched their ponies to the gate-posts, Max was being dragged around by Crackers.

'You can let go of Patchy, he'll stay with Minstrel,' I told him, as, with Snowman trotting beside me, I ran towards the farm buildings. Angela had already disappeared into the long, low one which faced us, so I turned left handed and ran towards another cluster by the big Dutch barn.

'Sukey, I'm going to check the caravan,' Chris shouted. 'I think I heard a dog barking there, and the fire's getting very close.'

'OK,' I replied. I had found two very new-looking loose-boxes standing on their own and over one half-door a grey head tossed, wild with excitement; the other box was empty – the bay stallion hadn't come back. I looked through the open doors into the wooden walled, peat floored barn, it had been converted into a covered school and it was empty. I ran round the other side, the buildings there held only hay and straw. I headed back to the main yard.

'Have you found a tack room?' I shouted to Angela. 'I need a headcollar.'

'The foals are wearing theirs, but I can't get them to lead. Do come and help, Sukey.' Angela's voice sounded desperate.

The building she was in looked as though it had been a byre. The foals were penned at one end with barricades of hurdles and straw bales. Chestnut and dun, they were both wearing proper foal headstalls. Angela, red in the face with heat and hurry, was trying to drag them out of the pen.

'I don't think they've ever been taught to lead, they only rear and run backwards. We're never going to get them away in time,' she moaned.

'Hang on a minute, I expect they'll follow Snowman,' I had seen a makeshift feed store and tack room at the other end of the byre. Snowman jogged after me as I ran to look for a headcollar. I found a collection piled on a cornbin and grabbed one about the right size for the grey head. Then I saw two webbing lead reins and grabbed them too.

'Here,' I tossed one to Angela, and, leaning over the side of the pen, buckled the other on the ring at the back of the dun foal's headstall. 'Now, see if they'll follow Snowman.' Snowman, who was behaving in a remarkably calm and obliging manner, looked back as I led him out of the byre and gave a tactful little whinny. Chris appeared through the mist of smoke, trotting up on Joey, carrying a bewildered looking Jack Russell terrier under one arm.

The caravan was locked too. I had to break the glass in the door with a brick. 'I think we ought to get moving. Danny and Huw are connecting up a hose, but it's pointless, one hose isn't going to stop that fire.'

The foals were emerging from the byre in a series of jerky rushes. I left Chris to help Angela and ran to collect the dapple-grey. He was charging round his box, neighing in a fierce, stallion voice and lashing out at the walls with his heels. I understood his alarm, for clouds of grey smoke were eddying round the yard and the air was full of the acrid scent of fire. Sneezing and half-blinded by watering eyes, I bundled Snowman into the next door stable and advanced on the stallion. He was only about fourteen-three, but in his explosive state he looked very formidable, and, without the greater danger of the fire, I doubt whether I would have been brave enough to corner him, sling the headcollar rope round his neck and haul him to a halt. Then, standing on tiptoe, I tried to slip the headcollar on his high-held head. I forced myself to talk soothingly as he flung himself about, ramming me against the wall and trampling on my toes. I began to think I would never get it on; that I would have to let him go loose and hope he could make his own escape. Outside the smoke had thickened and I could hear Chris calling me, a desperate note in his voice. Then, suddenly, the stallion gave in, and remaining still for a moment, allowed me to buckle the strap. I left him in his box while I mounted Snowman, then opened his door and let him plunge kicking and squealing into the smoke-filled yard. My watering eyes were refusing to see properly and with the stallion prancing and bucking I was being pulled out of the saddle and my arm half out of its socket. Huw

appeared, 'Is that the only horse you've found?' he asked.

'Yes, except for the foals. Is the fire-brigade coming?'

'Yes, we got them and the police. *And* we found a cat in the house.' He waved a holdall at me and my watering eyes observed the face of an indignant Persian cat looking out of the unzipped end. 'The others have taken the foals and the dog into the field behind these buildings, there's less smoke there; shall I lead the way?'

We trotted across the yard and through a gate, I concentrated grimly on the headcollar rope, I had to hang on to it somehow; if I let go there was no way of knowing what the stallion would do, in his frenzied mood I could see him galloping straight into the flames.

'Can you shut the gate?' I shouted to Huw as soon as we were in the field. 'I may not be able to hang on much longer.'

The stallion had seen the other ponies and dragged me towards them, he suddenly looked noble instead of frenzied, as, pricking his ears and arching his neck, he approached them at a slow, cadenced trot. Snowman, as obliging as ever, kept pace with him.

'Now we've got all the animals out oughtn't some of us to go back and try to stop the fire?' asked Angela.

'Huw and I tried,' answered Danny, dragging a squealing Crackers away from the stallion. 'We found a tap and connected up a hose, but there was no pressure, the water just trickled out, useless.'

'The farm wouldn't be on the mains, not right out here. I expect the water's just piped from some nearby spring,' added Huw, 'and it's probably dried up in the drought.'

'But if there's no water the fire-brigade won't be able to do anything when they get here,' I said, no longer able to keep the desperation from my voice.

'I suppose they'll bring a tankful of water or foam with them, but I don't think they are going to be in time to save the farm,' Huw sounded deeply sad.

'The smoke's getting thicker every minute, let's start looking for a weak place in the boundary wall,' said Angela as a gust of smoke-laden wind hit us, blowing particles of ash into our eyes.

'Head over towards Menacoell,' instructed Danny. 'Wind's coming from the southwest now.'

I had gritty bits of ash in both eyes and no spare hand with which to wipe them, so, temporarily blinded, I had to rely on Snowman to follow the other ponies.

Suddenly we were out of the choking, blinding smoke and the relief was terrific.

'Can some one hold this idiot for a minute while I get the bits out of my eyes,' I called plaintively. Huw gave the cat to Max and came to my rescue. The others seemed preoccupied with the fire and, when I could see again I knew why. Now we were out of the path of the smoke we had a clear view of the farmhouse and the hungry flames raging in its garden. The yard gate seemed to be burning too and beyond it, in the far corner of the yard, a thick spiral of darker smoke rose.

'That's where the caravan is,' said Chris pointing, 'there's a woodstack near it and what looked like old tractor oil in a drum, and spilt on the ground. I knew it would go up, it only needed one spark over the wall. At least you're safe,' he told the terrier.

'Where is that fire-brigade? They've been hours,' complained Angela.

'I hope we found all the animals,' said Max in a worried voice.

'Well, we've done our best,' answered Danny, 'And it's a good thing Mr Spalding's only just moved in and there aren't many to rescue. What would we have done if there had been a pig unit, or a couple of thousand chickens?'

'Don't talk about it,' said Angela. We stood watching in fascinated horror as the flames licked hungrily round the sides of the house. Even the ponies were appalled; Crackers stopped twirling and the dappled stallion stood like a statue, staring with his huge brown Arab eyes.

I was telling myself that we'd better get going, had better start looking for a weak place in the boundary wall, start tearing out stones before we found ourselves trapped, when Angela exclaimed, 'Look, people!' We all turned to see a land-rover being driven at high speed along the track from the Crooked Billet, it was lurching and leaping perilously as it tore over the rough ground.

'Looks like Mr Spalding's land-rover,' said Danny, 'he's not going to try to reach the farm, is he?'

'Yes, he thinks the animals are still there; he'll try to rescue them,' Chris's voice was shaking.

'He'll be burned to death,' wailed Angela. For a moment we looked at each other aghast. Then Huw said, 'We must tell him quickly. Snowman's the best jumper, Sukey, and he's the fastest.'

'OK. Here, hang on to Dapple.' I was looking round, making a plan. I could have jumped straight over the wall on to the moor but winding sheep paths, muddling their way through rocky outcrops and heather, are useless for fast riding, so I set off at a gallop, heading for the wall into the smaller field, the one directly behind the house. Snowman seemed to sense the sudden need for urgency and I forgot the hard ground now that we had a human life to save. We flew over the wall and I sent him into a flat-out gallop We *had* to reach the track and stop Mr Spalding, prevent him from making a reckless dash into

the house to save the cat, stop him going into the caravan or yard. We were back in the path of the smoke now. Coughing and wiping my streaming eyes with the back of one hand, I was forced to slow down, it was no use riding faster than I could see. I tried shouting, 'Wait, Mr Spalding. Wait, we've rescued them. The animals are safe,' I called between bouts of coughing. But I knew that the wind was carrying my words away and the roar and crackle of the fire was drowning them. I steadied Snowman. The boundary wall was high and solid, I had never jumped such a fearsome-looking one before. I wondered if I was asking too much of Snowman, if he could see it clearly through the smoke. For a moment I thought of pulling up, of attempting to call to Mr Spalding from the field side of the wall, but calling wouldn't be enough, I had to stop him and there wasn't a second to lose. I gathered up my courage and tried to impart it through my legs and reins as I alerted Snowman to the wall ahead. 'Come on, boy,' I shouted as I rode at it, ready for the landing, ready to turn him along the track. Then we were on the moor, a blackened waste, still smouldering. I looked for the land-rover, it had stopped on the edge of the fire and two people were running down the track, Mr Spalding and a girl. She was crying, he was trying to put on a macintosh as he ran.

Snowman and I barred their way. 'It's all right,' I said, 'we've saved the animals,' but my words were drowned by a new noise, a great blast of aircraft noise and there, coming from the direction of Redbridge, was a helicopter. It passed low above our heads, deafening us and terrifying Snowman, then it hovered over the house and seemed to be emptying the contents of a giant scoop or bucket it carried over the roof and down the sides of the house. Then it flew over the yard and loosed gallons more of its sticky-looking foam on the buildings and the pile of timber before whirling away, back towards Redbridge.

'That's damped it down a bit, I'll be able to get into the house now,' said Mr Spalding, in a shocked, despairing voice.

'We got the cat out, a grey Persian cat,' I told him. 'My friends are looking after her over there in the field.'

Mr Spalding began to say something but his voice was drowned by the repetitive, double yowl of sirens, and racing along the track from the Crooked Billet came three fire-engines. Mr Spalding ran to move the land-rover which he had left blocking the track.

'They're too late,' sobbed the girl. 'What's the good of coming now, when Corky's burned to death.'

'We got a dog out of the caravan,' I told her. 'And a grey stallion out of the stable.'

'You got a dog out of the caravan? But you couldn't, it was locked,' sobbed the girl. 'I left it locked, if only I hadn't gone to those beastly revels. Poor little Corky.'

'Look, we got a Jack Russell type of terrier out of the caravan,' I shouted, as I dragged her and led Snowman out of the fire-engines' way.

'You mean you've saved Corky? He's not dead.' She gazed at me with an expression of disbelief.

'If he's the terrier who was in the caravan by the woodstack,' I answered, hoping that there were no more caravans hidden among the farm buildings. 'My brother heard him barking and broke in. But are there any *more* animals anywhere?' I went on trying to control my impatience, 'We found a cat in the house, the dog in the caravan, a dapple-grey stallion and two foals in the stables. Is that the lot?'

'Yes, I think so. Mr Spalding,' she called, but he was busy directing the firemen towards the stables. One engine was pumping water and foam on the house, the second had just loosed its cascade on the smouldering remains of the woodstack and the still-blazing caravan, two men from the third engine were clearing away the charred remnants of the five-barred gate. As they drove into the yard I grabbed Mr Spalding. 'Please listen,' I said trying to break through to his stunned mind, 'We were riding over the moor and saw the fire. Some of us telephoned from your house and rescued the cat while the others rescued the dog from the caravan, the grey stallion and the foals. They're all over there in the field. Look.' As the smoke was dying down it was possible to see again, and coming across the field was a group of riders. They were led by the prancing grey stallion, who was towing Huw and a very cross-looking Minstrel. Chris was carrying the dog, Max the cat, while Angela and Danny each led a lagging foal.

Mr Spalding stared at them, he still seemed only half aware, but then he said, 'Thank God,' with great feeling and I knew it had sunk in at last. The girl had given a cry of joy and climbing the field wall, ran to meet the riders. I heard her crying, 'Corky, Corky,' as she ran.

Suddenly the moor was alive with people, armed with fire-brooms, spades and shovels. They advanced across the vast blackened stretch, beating out any still-smouldering pockets of fire. The police were there too, organising the parking of land-rovers and trucks, and then the helicopter returned and, flying along the edges of the fire, spilled its foaming load on the still unburnt grass and heather. It was under control, I thought with relief, as I mounted. Then a giant spot of water landed on my hand. I thought it was from a fire-hose until I looked up and saw that the huge black storm clouds were now right overhead. And, as I looked, the storm broke; a great torrent of rain beat down on the parched moor and a cheer went up from the fire-fighters as the hot ashes sizzled and the pockets of fire in the grass and heather faltered and went out.

7

A question of economics

Dripping wet, most of us had taken refuge in the long building. We had tied our ponies to the rings and window-bars and were trying to persuade the foals back into their pen when Mum and Dad appeared, looking extraordinarily dry and clean.

Mum gave a cry of horror at our appearances, 'Are you all right? No burns or anything?' she asked anxiously.

'Fine,' we answered, and slapping the dun foal's rump, I asked, 'How did you know we were here?'

'The police telephoned, apparently Danny told them you were with him when he reported the fire,' Mum explained.

'And they took over the public address at the revels,' added Dad. 'They announced that North Moor was on fire and Quarry Farm threatened. Luckily they had the sense to give the fire-engines a start because the Crooked Billet lane is now solid with traffic.'

'The police thought we might be useful, they expected some animal casualties,' Mum went on, 'but I gather you got all the livestock away in time.'

'There weren't many of them to get away,' Chris sounded casual.

'No problem,' agreed Danny.

'You didn't have to rescue the foals,' protested Angela. 'It took me ages to catch them and then they didn't know how to lead. They're still wild.'

'Well they're back now,' I said when Chris had helped me heave the reluctant dun into the pen. I shut the hurdle gate and fastened the wire loop securely. 'Now what about Dapple?'

'His name is Desert Magic,' said Chris as we went out to the yard, 'and he's a registered part-bred Arab. Corky's owner told me. She's the new girl groom and *her* name is Jackie.'

'Well Desert Magic is pulling Huw's arms out of their sockets,' I answered, full of fellow-feeling, 'so we'd better find somewhere to put him.'

'I've looked in the stallion boxes, they're both awash with fire-brigade water and sticky with helicopter goo; he can't go in there,' objected Huw.

'We'd better ask Jackie or Mr Spalding where we can put him,' I said, looking round.

'They're busy. I don't mind holding him and I'm so wet I can't be any wetter,' argued Huw cheerfully.

'Did you know that the helicopter's bucket holds a hundred gallons of foam?' asked Chris. 'Apparently it's quite a new invention, they scoop up the water from the estuary or the sea, tip in the special sticky detergent stuff and that's it. One of the firemen told me about it; it's great in forest fires because the foam sticks to the trees and then they don't burn.'

'Sounds terrific,' said Huw hanging on to the head-collar rope as the bored, wet stallion caprioled round him.

I could see Jackie who, assisted by Mrs Webber and Kelly, seemed to be sorting through the black soggy mess which had once been a caravan, but I decided on Mr Spalding, who was only watching helplessly as the firemen threw charred curtains down from his fire-blackened windows. The others followed me across the yard. The rain had slackened to a drizzle and the acrid smell of the wet black ashes was almost overpowering. Out on the moor the fire-fighters were beginning to head for home. Several of the cars were bogged down and the sounds of frustrated engines and spinning wheels filled the air. Mr Jackson and Mr Webber joined us, black and dripping like the rest of us they seemed to be enjoying themselves.

'Now that is a nice 'orse,' announced Mr Jackson, standing back to admire Desert Magic. 'I could have him over at my place for a few days if they've nowhere to put him.'

'But you've already got Goldie in one of your loose-boxes,' I reminded him. 'And you couldn't put him next to a mare.'

'Doesn't sound as though we'll have the little chestnut much longer; seems she's got to be put down. Mr King's taking young Jess back to France and he fairly bit your Ma's head off when she rang him, said there was no way in which he was going to change his mind.'

We looked at each other miserably. We'd completely forgotten Goldie while we'd been occupied with the fire, and now it seemed as though her fate had been decided without us.

'We must do something,' Max appealed to his father. 'We can't just let her be killed.'

'It's a question of economics, that's what's wrong with the world. We ought to be ruled by compassion, but it always comes down to economics in the end. Economics and greed,' answered Mr Webber in a very bitter voice.

I had managed to attract Mr Spalding's attention and he came over to us. Now that his lightweight suit was wet and shapeless and his face streaked with grime, he had stopped looking like a bank-manager, but he still didn't look the least like a farmer. I explained that we'd put the foals back in their pen but that both the stallion boxes were waterlogged, and asked if there was somewhere else we could put Desert Magic.

'I wonder what sort of condition the Dutch barn is in?' he said when he had thought for a moment. 'We've made it into a covered exercise area. He'd be safe enough there until the boxes dry out; I'll come with you and see.

I can't begin to tell you how grateful I am,' he went on, as we crossed the yard, squelching through water and foam. 'The full horror of what *might* have happened hasn't sunk in yet.'

'That's all right,' Danny broke in quickly. 'Just a bit of luck we were passing at the right moment.'

'We expected to find more horses,' said Angela, craftily seizing her chance. 'We thought you had a bay stallion too; I looked everywhere for him.'

'You mean No Omen; we moved him on a couple of days ago,' answered Mr Spalding evenly.

'There was a lot of talk about that bay 'orse,' said Mr Jackson, who had attached himself to our party. 'That groom of his was always hinting he knew something the rest of us didn't, folk never knew what to believe.'

'Yes, I gathered that something of that sort was going on,' Mr Spalding allowed a faint note of indignation to creep into his voice. 'I knew one member of the syndicate which owns the horse and, since it was the end of the season and they were roughing him off, I agreed to him coming here for a couple of months. It turned out to be an error of judgement,' he admitted primly. 'I was told that he had failed at stud and was coming here prior to being gelded and then tried over hurdles.' Mr Spalding took off his spectacles and wiped the lenses slowly. 'When I moved down here, rather earlier than expected, I found a

stream of barren mares arriving from all over the country, their owners apparently under the misapprehension
that the horse was not No Omen but his better-known
brother, the kidnapped Derby winner Easter Chance,
smuggled into this country by the criminals who had
kidnapped him. Not at all the sort of thing I like to be
mixed up with,' he added, a look of distaste on his black,
streaked face.

'But the horse did come from Ireland, we saw him
arrive; he was in the hold of a boat in Pennecford
harbour,' objected Angela.

'Yes, I am afraid that some members of the syndicate
were prepared to stoop to all kinds of deception to bring
in business,' Mr Spalding explained carefully. 'You see,
No Omen had failed completely on the race-track so,
naturally, his services as a sire were not in demand, the
breeders didn't want his foals. But the syndicate were
desperate for stud fees, so *they* put about the rumours that
he was Easter Chance and sent him along the coast by
boat – he was previously stabled in Dorset – to give
credence to their rumours.'

'You mean that they were hoping people would spot
him being unloaded at midnight?' asked Huw. 'They
were trying to stir up as much suspicion as possible?'

'Yes, I believe that to be the case,' agreed Mr Spalding
primly.

Mr Jackson burst into roars of laughter. 'Best thing
I've heard for months,' he spluttered, rocking on his feet.
'And it's true enough. That lad of yours, Lenny, was
always whispering and hinting. Wouldn't I love to see
the owners' faces when they find they rushed their old
mares down here for nothing!'

'Lenny O'Brien was no employee of mine, he came
with the horse,' Mr Spalding corrected him.

'And you're absolutely certain that it was No Omen who was here?' Chris asked Mr Spalding, 'they look very alike. You're quite sure that he didn't have ermine marks on his near hind sock?'

Mr Spalding smiled frostily. 'I can see you've done your homework, but I can assure you that I also had the horse's markings checked out very thoroughly.'

'And now you'll have this grey fellow standing at stud next year?' asked Mr Jackson, controlling his laughter and giving Desert Magic a hearty slap on the neck.

'Yes, I bought him with that intention. Now I've retired I thought I'd try my hand at breeding ponies, larger ponies; thirteen hands to fourteen-two. I thought a half-bred Arab would cross well with the local ponies.'

'Ah, now, we know just the little mare for you. She's looking for a good home on account of an accident,' Mr Jackson gave me a friendly wink. 'Chestnut, about thirteen-one. She'll make a grand little brood mare.'

Mr Spalding began to say something about not buying stock at the moment, but Angela interrupted quickly, 'She's the pony who had the accident on the cattle grid, do you remember we telephoned from your house. Oh, do please say you'll have her.'

'Trouble is that Jess, the girl who broke her collarbone, bought the pony without asking her parents,' Danny explained, 'and now her father won't let her keep Goldie. He says she's got to be destroyed.'

'We must find her a good home quickly, but the problem is that she's got these badly-broken knees.'

'One knee is worse than the other and it's just possible that she won't be one hundred per cent sound, but that wouldn't matter if she was a brood mare.' We were all explaining, all looking at Mr Spalding hopefully, but he seemed more interested in the state of the Dutch barn.

'Not too bad at all,' he decided. 'I think we'll leave his headcollar on. If you would just unclip the rope,' he asked Huw politely. Desert Magic began to canter round, snorting and showing off. He looked so lovely, but I was thinking of poor Goldie standing miserably in the Jackson stable with hanging head and swollen knees. She might never be able to canter round like that again. She might not even live long enough for her knees to stop hurting.

'We could look after Goldie for another week or two,' Huw was saying, 'and we can club together to pay for her food, if only we knew that she had somewhere to go at the end of the holidays, when we start school.'

'I can see that there's a danger of Quarry Farm becoming a rest home for lame ponies and orphaned foals,' said Mr Spalding with a frosty smile. 'And the suitability of a mare for breeding is more complicated than you think. Is she the right age? And, if she's getting on, has she had a foal before? But I'll tell you what I will do, if you can look after her for two or three more days while we sort out our problems here, I'll give her a home for the winter. I'd like an older pony to run with the foals, and then in the spring, we can reconsider her case and decide on her future career.'

'Oh, thank you *very* much.'

'That's great!'

'It's a perfect solution,' we were looking at each other with a mixture of delight and relief, 'and she has a very sweet nature, she'll like looking after the foals.'

Max was shouting the good news to Kelly; Chris rushed to tell Mum and Dad. Goldie's future settled, Mr Jackson was offering Mr Spalding two of his old caravans on hire as temporary housing.

'He's offered to *lend* us one if the cottage isn't finished in time for the winter,' Max muttered to me. 'But as he's offered to teach Dad to thatch and to help him build up the walls once the harvest's over, Dad's going to help him with the corn and fix up some electric lights in the tack room and stables in exchange. They seem to have been bartering away all the time they were beating out the fire.'

We collected our ponies, and Huw had heaved Kelly up on Patchy and was pulling up her stirrups when Mum, who had come to see us off, said, 'It's such a shame that both Webbers can't ride at once, we must try and find another pony. Would they be good enough for Bingo, Sukey? I mean in the term, when Angela's not here.'

'They should be in another week or two,' I answered, 'especially Max, who's got the longest legs.'

Angela gave a despairing moan. 'You're all so lucky living here. Why can't I live on the moor and ride darling

Bingo at the weekends? It's not fair that I have to go home and listen to all that boring boat talk.'

'It's not *all* fun,' Huw told her ruefully. He had taken off his tee-shirt and was wringing it out.

'It's not a bit like we expected, is it, Max?' said Kelly.

'No, we thought a moor would be quiet and peaceful, a lazy sort of life with not much going on,' Max admitted, 'but it seems to be one long drama, only you're not a watcher you're suddenly part of it, and quite an important part too.'

'Oh, it's not a bad place,' said Danny, 'and things 'll settled down now that Jess has gone and the drought's over.'